The Mournful Threads

By
Kevin Trusty

Edited by Denise Baran-Unland
Cover art by Molly Errek
Creative contributions by Todd M. Calcaterra
ISBN: 978-1-7356544-4-7

Contents

Exegesis

Long ago, there was a message – a warning of what's to come.

But too few listened. Of those who believed, many still refused to accept what was in plain sight.

Now, a confluence has begun.

Storms. Wars and threats of wars. Greed. Disease. A world whose very stewards encourage its end.

Conflict has become normal. Accidents orchestrated. Nations tearing themselves apart from within. Humanity is drowning in violence and mistrust.

The duality of human nature to create and destroy is confounding. But then, they are in his image.

Existence itself is tragic. Nations and empires achieve their marvels while standing on the shoulders of death and sacrifice. When finally, at the zenith of possibility, when tranquility should be within reach, they've let it slip away.

It is ironic that the pursuit of what they should desire is what heralds the end.

Duality, indeed.

Part of existence is understanding that which is not to be understood.

The truth has always been the greatest lie.

He is still here.

Widow's Walk

A throng of passengers jammed the platform, rushing to hop on the awaiting train.

Men in finely tailored suits wove through the crowd, leading equally well-dressed ladies by hand, and helping them board the last passenger car. The conductor issued the final boarding call. It was 9:50 in the morning and the renowned Eastern Star sat strong and imposing on the tracks, ready to make another speedy run.

The crew scurried in and out of the train, busy with their final pre-trip checks.

"William?" A tall, wiry man called out as he gracefully hopped up the three steps into the oil-stained cab of the venerable locomotive.

"Yes! You must be Peter. Glad to meet you," William said, extending a hand.

He winced at the young man's cold, iron-strong grip.

"Likewise. I understand it's not common to switch firemen at the last second, but I'm looking forward to working with you." Peter nodded. "Old Lyle Fedler back at the office speaks highly of you. I hear it's your last time out as engineer?"

William Hargrove had been a train engineer for Wyndish & Redding Railway for almost 10 years, but when the chance to manage part of the company's westward expansion fell into his lap, he couldn't refuse. As a bonus, he'd no longer have to deal with his asshole of a managing engineer, Reginald Smythe. William respected Mr. Smythe's longevity in the industry, but he felt the boss was little more than a greedy curmudgeon who should've retired years ago and only stayed working to feed his bottomless ego. William couldn't stand to work for him any longer. He was even more excited about spending three whole weeks at home with his beloved Caroline in their new house before starting the new job.

"Fedler needs to lay off the whiskey!" William laughed. "He should go back to the circus with the rest of his clan. Nah, he's a good fellow. But yes, I'm getting off the rails and into the office. Time for something new."

Another crewman entered the cab, cueing up William to make the introduction. "This here is Robert Lang, our brakeman."

The burly brake operator stepped forward, offering a hand. Peter took it and clasped his other hand over it. "Great to meet you, sir!"

"Welcome aboard the Eastern Star!"

Peter smiled wide. "I've heard a lot about her. She's famous, eh?"

"Well, she should be. Eleven years without a scratch," Robert said with a proud grin. "Hopefully one more to go." He nudged his conductor. "Should be no sweat, as long as Billy here doesn't slouch today."

William chewed his lip. He never thought he'd miss driving trains until people started saying it out loud. He couldn't shake the bothersome feeling about leaving, even though it was good for him and Caroline.

"Get back to it, boyo," William chided. Robert gave a friendly laugh as he exited the cab to resume his brake tests.

Peter looked around the cab. "If I may ask, William, why step down? This seems like a wonderful duty. And you must be a swell engineer to drive the Eastern Star!"

"Wife and I moved into a new house out in the country earlier this year, and I'm ready to spend more time at home. How about you? Been a fireman long?"

"My first trip!" Peter said, beaming. "Finished training last week."

"And before that?"

Peter turned and looked out the window, murmuring something that William couldn't quite make out.

"Kid?"

"Oh, sorry. I did some travelling. Odd jobs here and there. Carpentry. Bricklaying. Things like that. Nothing too exciting. But trains! Now, trains are exciting! And how about this? It's your last run and my first. That should make for some kind of luck!" He winked.

William forced a laugh. He appreciated the enthusiasm, but he wondered if this young man could handle the Star's hefty equipment on a speed run. Every fireman he ever knew took several long runs to get the hang of it, especially on an older train like this. They can be a little temperamental.

The day before yesterday, Mr. Smythe surprised William by transferring his fireman for no apparent reason. "Company policy," according to the telegram. Of course. It was the umbrella term that William hated, an excuse for management's excuses. Although crew changes throughout the company were common lately, William would've appreciated more than a day's notice. But as he considered this, he reasoned maybe it's good timing. If the boss keeps shaking things up, he'd be better off getting out of the engineer's seat.

"Well, even better luck is the robin's nest we found under the inboard right rear wheel yesterday morning." William couldn't contain his grin. "It was empty, but the big birds were circling. One even landed on the depot roof about an hour ago. God gave us a great day."

Peter's perpetual smile dropped like a stone; his golden eyes flashed with intensity.

William feigned concern as he eyed his new coworker. New firemen were usually of a younger sort, but Peter came off as a little more seasoned. His tangled, silver-blonde locks and lean build gave him a youthful appearance, but he carried an air of wisdom in his eyes.

William wondered about Peter's background. Or if he knew about running a train at all. "This…this'll be one for the books, then, Peter. We seem ready. Why don't you go through your final checks?

"You bet!" Peter gave a quick clap as he snapped to work, preparing his station as ordered. William watched the man check his dials and all the fire equipment. "Looks like the fire should be ready to light. No ash, which is good. Box is set. Starter kindling looks good." He flicked a finger on a few gauges above the controls "And the water is ready."

William nodded, impressed.

"Okay then. I finished all the route prep and timetables. Everything is in order."

"Swell!" the new fireman replied. Peter patted the top of the regulator. "This sure seems like a strong old train. Just you wait. We'll be flying in no time!"

Normally the run from eastern New York through to Pittsburgh was uneventful; a generally straight spur-less shot with only one large rise and no stops. Just the kind of lazy run he'd be glad to end on, William thought. But with the new crewman, he might at least have some interesting conversation.

"We just may," William said. "Although part of me wants to milk it, being my last run and all. I might miss being onboard."

"You have *no idea* how true that is going to be," Peter said, his tone suddenly serious and flat.

William blinked. "I'm sorry?"

Peter just smirked at the retiring engineer. After a pause, William turned, trying to distract himself from the awkward look by re-checking his dials again. "What was that about truth?" he asked again after a few seconds.

"Oh, nothing," Peter resumed his joviality. "I only meant we—*we*— have no idea what kind of life awaits us when we…change jobs. Like me, William. I never thought I'd end up working for Wyndish & Redding after where I came from."

Finally, the box William was curious to open. "And where was that exactly?"

William studied him carefully; hopeful that Peter's reply might shed light on his appearance. He looked young but his confident expressions and fluid body language indicated experience beyond his years. Beyond mere bricklaying and carpentry.

Peter lazily shrugged with a smile, as if hinting at some accomplishment.

"We can talk about *that* on the way, sir."

William flipped his tarnished bronze pocket watch, then nodded at Peter as he clapped it shut. The rookie lit the firebox, preparing the engine for travel. Satisfied that Peter knew his way around, William doublechecked the injectors, tested the boiler water level, switched on his lamps, and verified the coal supply—duties he'd already performed twice each.

At a quarter past ten o'clock, the 150-passenger steamer began to inch away from the wooden structure of the depot toward Pittsburgh.

"Here we go." William sighed as his big train rolled for the last time with him in charge, gaining steam away from the metropolis of New York City and out toward the awaiting fields. As the city shrank in the distance behind them, the sunlit morning sky suddenly shifted. A wall of heavy clouds, pregnant with rain, roiled up right in their path.

~ * ~

Twenty minutes later, they were a full six minutes ahead of schedule. Thick raindrops pelted the window of the cab as the train roared westward toward Pittsburgh. A few cars behind the cab, some passengers mingled in the bar, smoking cigars, and sipping coffee and overpriced brandy. Others retreated to private quarters further back.

Peter watched the dials at the fire control station with strict concentration, while William stared ahead, making sure the train stayed true on the rails. Robert tested the brakes with a quick pull of the lever, satisfied when the locomotive slowed in response. The cab swayed steadily. The floorboards popped at rhythmic intervals as the train's massive wheels spun along the tracks. Everything was in perfect working condition. William loved trips like this, even in a storm. He knew the relatively straight road to Pittsburgh only had one climb to navigate. He thumbed open his pocket watch again.

"Still well ahead. Let's see if we can really beat the clock on this one. Give her a little more!" William shouted above the powerful metal noise as the Eastern Star picked up steam. He smiled despite the nasty weather. He knew this run — every curve, every notch on the track. He wanted to make this one memorable. William stared at his watch, silently counting each tick. When he had the cadence down, he checked it against his rail map under the yellow glow of the lamp. A hill was coming. He snapped the watch shut then turned to check that Peter had heard him.

"You got it!" Peter shouted, adjusting the controls at his station and then tossing more shovelfuls of coal into the piping hot chute. Although it was still midmorning, the merciless rain and anvil thunderclouds covered the area in a hazy dusk. Lamplight flickered like a haunted golden strobe in each cabin, but the ride was so smooth the passengers seemed not to notice or care. The hefty, 16-car machine barreled forward with great speed, as if daring the thunderstorm to give its best shot. Almost in response, lightning cracked silver across the sky and the driving rain turned to hail.

William ignored the intensifying storm outside and monitored his engine's performance. Despite the nasty weather, this felt like the fastest run he'd ever made. The Eastern Star practically glided along the tracks. Even the deck vibrations were barely noticeable. A perfect way to end this job, he realized. The minutes ticked by without interruption. Ever the professional, he tried to peer ahead at the tracks through the downpour before the comfortable thrum lulled him into carelessness.

From timing his watch along with the distances on the map, William knew they were approaching the climb ahead—one he felt prepared to take with the extra speed. As they raced closer to the rising slope, William smiled confidently. The gauges were all in their optimal ranges, accompanied by the satisfying chugs of healthy locomotive horsepower.

Suddenly, the outside door slid open.

"Understand this!" Peter shouted, jarring William from his proud stupor as he stepped into the cabin. He was drenched.

He twirled a long section of thick rubber hose in his grease-caked hands. Through the playful spinning, William could see it was frayed at both ends. "I like trains, William."

William stepped toward the fireman.

"Where did you go—is that—" William shouted. "How could you tear out part of the brake hose while we're running? And in the name of God, *why?*"

"I like small places, too." Peter massaged his chin, as if in thought, smearing dark grease along his jawline. "Like that silent town in Pennsylvania, Crystal-something or other? Boy, *that's* a good fall from the bridge down to the river."

William leaned back into the tilt of the cab, steadying himself on his worktable as the train began to run up the hill. "Did you hear me, Peter? What have you done?"

He reached out to snatch the hose away from Peter, who yanked it behind his back like a teasing schoolchild.

"They're rebuilding that bridge as we speak, of course," Peter said, examining the section of hose as if studying how it worked. "I had one of my friends go over there to keep an eye on the place, and those moronic townsfolk, for me. Flies to the spider and all that."

"What are you babbling about?"

"You see William, in the very short time since we've met, I've figured you out." He giggled through closed lips. "More accurately, I've known you your whole life. Your eyes are always on the prize, unaware or uncaring of who or what is pulling your strings, even when they're right in front of you."

Peter strolled around the small cab, drizzling fluid from the ripped hose; he spun it between his fingers, smiling all the while. "Despite always watching for the endgame, you're easily…distracted. You do not know what Wyndish & Redding are truly about, but *I* do. You might say I have an eye for greed and pride that is unrivaled by any man. Not that you apply, you're a good boy. But my job is to notice such things."

The bastard is enjoying himself, William thought. The deck pitched forward like a ship on the sea as the train gained speed on the downward slope of the hill. With his attention fully on Peter, William didn't notice the approaching signal at the switch. The Eastern Star rolled right through it, toward an unfinished spur line.

"When I see those traits so strongly in others, I'm compelled to intervene. I can't allow too many people to do my work for me—not yet at least. But you sure all have been trying. Just like a train, you see, I have to keep the game going on schedule. No shortcuts. Besides, what's a little misfortune compared to centuries of manipulation and deceit? Maybe one of these not so accidental accidents will stop Wyndish & Redding once and for all. Then again, maybe not. It sure gets His scrutiny one way or another."

William had had enough. "Who's scrutiny? What the hell are you talking about? You're crazy, mister!" he screamed.

Peter tilted his head, eyes fixed on William, a slight curl in his top lip.

The outer door slid open again. "William! We missed the switch! We're going much too fast!" Robert shouted as he climbed back into the cab. "We've got to slow down or kill it!"

"Hmm. Interesting choice of words, Robert." Peter crossed his arms. "Do you know how legends begin, William? They all start out as truth, you know. Now, who do you think begins that truth?"

William opened his mouth to speak, then snapped it shut.

Peter tossed the torn brake hose on the floor and wiped his hands on his coveralls. "I think I'll journey on to Pittsburgh myself, lads. I might even stay awhile and try that new ball game everyone is raving about. You know of it? Looks like fun. Well, anyway, perhaps I'll see some of you soon." He turned toward the door.

William pounded his fists against the steel wall of the cab.

"Hey! What does that *mean*? Help stop this thing!"

Peter spun back and smiled at him. William was sick of that smile. "You see?" Peter shook his head, pointing toward the controls. "It is so easy to ensnare a man with the slightest distraction."

"Shut it down, William! Shut the engine down, now!" Robert screamed. But it was too late. The train kept thundering downhill on the incomplete spur line.

"As I said, I have a thing for tinkering with trains."

With a casual wave, Peter stepped out of the speeding cab, and disappeared into the foggy storm.

William stood motionless in shock. Robert blinked his own confusion away and resumed yanking and pulling on the levers, begging the brakes to catch, but it was no use. The train sped forward and jumped the gap in the rails at maximum speed. Its momentum carried it off the tracks at such a severe angle that windows in each car shattered from the violent twisting. Glassware and luggage crashed to the floor. Passengers screamed and fell about, unable to brace themselves against the jarring force of the derailment. And then everything went still and soft, as if they were floating.

In the cab of the Eastern Star, William watched hopelessly as the murky surface of the Delaware River grew closer in the small forward window.

~ * ~

It's not supposed to be this way, she told herself.

The first thing every morning and at least twice before nightfall, Caroline climbed the creaky, spiral staircase and stepped out onto the pinnacle, a full four stories up. There she stood, one hand clinging to the rusting iron railing more for comfort than balance, the other resting on her expecting belly.

She looked with longing brown eyes through the tree-lined fields at Hargrove Manor. *Their* fields.

Every day for the past three months, she came up here to wait and watch, believing the news was a lie.

~ * ~

Angels in Hell

Crash!

A sound like glass breaking came from just outside the door. Simon didn't even flinch. He sat exhausted, cross-legged upon a splintering rocker in a warm pool of mid-afternoon sunlight streaming in through the window. He held a smoldering cigar in one dirt-encrusted hand and a glass of bourbon in the other.

He rocked himself up, tamped out his stogie, and winced as he drained the rest of his stale whiskey in one gulp. He yanked open the door and stepped out to the sagging wooden porch, right onto the remains of a newly fallen icicle. The frozen shards were already slushing in the sunlight. Splotches of grass peeked through the snow and the crisp air soothed his lungs. He smirked and pushed up his sleeves as he scanned the bright, rolling expanse of his land. In another week, there'd be spring's budding leaves, green grass and high skies as far as the eye could see. God's land, he called it, still unblemished by the endeavors of westward expansion.

Squishy footsteps broke his moment of peace.

"Hey, when can we start? It's all melting!" a familiar voice bellowed from the side of the porch.

Simon snapped his eyes shut and gnashed his teeth. "Soon as the ground is thawed," he said to his friend John for what felt like the hundredth time. Simon ran his hands through his thick, graying hair. The tattered, dark blue coveralls he always wore hid a strong physique and accentuated a pair of sad, brown eyes. Simon wasn't the warmest person, not outwardly, at least. He was just content to keep to himself – and seize each opportunity to get ahead with an iron grasp. He told himself all winter that this new job at the cemetery would give him that chance.

"Come on in and have a drink," Simon said with reluctance, leaning toward the door. "Let's go over it one more time."

The two men ambled inside.

~ * ~

Remnants of winter's grip still hung in the air at night, but the strengthening mid-April sun during the day was an encouraging sign. The townsfolk of Swan River, in the hilly iron range of northern Minnesota, anticipated their return to the lush fields, forests, and mines. America was on the verge of prospering and, like everyone else in town, Simon Granville expected 1896 to be a rewarding year.

Handling standard burials was one of Simon's more interesting duties at Sago Cemetery. He enjoyed the challenge of digging perfectly square plots as though sculpting the earth. His other chores of landscaping and general maintenance were mundane by comparison. They felt too mindless for someone with his experience. It wasn't glamorous. He lived below his means, saving for the next big opportunity – a new house, maybe a venture out west. But this year was going to be different – the prospect of a new, special project as caretaker excited him more than he'd been in some time.

Wyndish & Redding Railway, a private and powerful transportation company founded by a couple of grinning, overweight New York tycoons, commissioned the project to install new railroads in the area. The deal with the Merritt family was to link with their Duluth, Missabe & Northern Railway Company and establish additional lines to the far west. With Rockefeller involved, the workers envisioned the dollars to practically fall from the sky. But to do this, they needed to cut through a significant segment of the cemetery's acreage. For Simon, this meant moving graves.

He accepted the additional work immediately. His contract outlined a rate at a price-per-grave-moved instead of a lump sum for the entire job. Simon would earn this pay on top of his standard salary – a strong raise for the year – even if he had to dig up the dead for it.

The cemetery project finally started on Thursday, May 12. Simon and his crew were more than eager to begin, and they arrived before sunrise to get a head start. Damp, spongy grass covered the muddy soil underneath – thick and heavy for several feet down. Backache conditions, but workable. They worked like this all day – digging, throwing, lifting, sweating. Simon stuck his shovel blade into the muck and rested a tired forearm on the handle. He sighed and removed his prized silver pocket watch: 5:34pm.

"All set?" he called out to his crew – four men he handpicked – who were hoisting up a wooden coffin with muddy ropes.

One of the workers, a young, red-haired southerner, clambered up out of a freshly dug hole. "Yeah, that's…six! Should we start on another?"

Simon looked up at the sun as it dipped beneath his horizon to rise on someone else's. He shook his head, smiling. "No, that's all for today. We'll pick back up here in the morning. Good first day!"

Simon nodded as he watched his ragtag crew of six pack up. It was a good group. They worked hard and complained little. He and John were the only full-time employees. Two were seasonal, only coming up from the south each year to escape the dreadful summer heat, and the other two were part-time night watchmen who weren't afraid to get dirty. He was glad they'd all be earning a little extra this year.

By the 26th of May, they had almost a third of the old graveyard dug up. Rotting coffins sat stacked atop the grass like giant firewood, awaiting their new plots. Late that Thursday afternoon, Simon was in the rickety old wooden tool shed just inside the cemetery's main entrance when the unmistakable squeal of the iron front gates swung open behind him. Robert Crowell, the land's owner, a portly, aging man with thinning hair the color of a storm cloud, had arrived. Simon was expecting the former clergyman-turned-businessman – it was their first payday from Wyndish & Redding.

"Your men sure work fast! At this rate you could have the whole cemetery moved in a month!"

The two men exchanged a friendly laugh and a strong handshake. "Just taking advantage of the good ground, Mr. Crowell."

"Christ on a crutch, call me Robert," he said, palms raised. "We've worked together forever it seems, and with this – ", he gestured toward the wall of coffins, "we're both going to cash in! We're in the right place at the right time, my boy. Speaking of, I have the first tally for you."

Robert pulled a leatherbound ledger out of his briefcase and handed it to Simon. Flipping to the bookmarked page, Simon's eyes grew wider as he read. His lips pursed. Robert stared at him in askance.

"This can't be right!" Simon yelled in surprise. "This doesn't even come out to a dollar per man on the crew! I thought we were in for some real decent bucks here!"

Robert glared at him and waived a finger in his direction. For all his friendliness, which Simon suspected was usually fake, Robert could change his mood by the minute.

"You agreed to the work. This is it. Did you not account for the number of graves?"

"Yes, of course I did!"

Robert shrugged as Simon checked the numbers again. And again. "Gosh, with the time this is taking away from our usual spring workload, it may as well be only a dime's worth." Robert chuckled softly. "But more is more, as they say, Sport!" Simon threw his arms up and stomped back toward the shed.

"Look, there may be more money for you when the job is complete," Robert called after him. "I heard them talking about bigger budgets and bonuses. These guys, they have deep pockets, you know."

Simon turned back and shoved the ledger into his rotund boss's chest. "For Christ's sake, Robert, something isn't right here. They're shorting us! It's less than what the contract said. And you can bet they're talking about their own bonuses, not ours. Talk to them!"

Long seconds passed between the two men. Finally, Robert nodded his understanding. He started to walk away, then paused, turning back to

Simon. "Time is money too. I'll see if I can grease the east coast fellas to sweeten the pot. Otherwise, you'll just have to find more graves to move."

Simon straightened. "What was that?"

"They're paying you per grave, right? Just keep at it – and don't cross the Lord! You used to be a priest, remember?"

The former preacher always had to throw a jab of a sermon to the former priest, Simon thought as he watched Robert shuffle toward the gate. He wondered how much Wyndish & Redding were paying *him*, and he didn't have to pick up a shovel.

~ * ~

Two more paydays went by without a penny of an increase.

One bright July morning, Simon sat in the tented field office at the east edge of the graveyard. He rubbed his stubbly chin, lazily scanning his cluttered desk for the cigar he left there yesterday. He dwelled on Robert's words from their last visit.

He stuck his head out of the tent and whistled, resting John's attention from his mortar work, and waved him over. John hustled in, sat across from Simon's desk and listened as Simon explained the issue he saw in Robert's ledger.

John raised both palms. "They're probably taking a cut. Or maybe they only listed the gross price on the contract. I'm sure there's tax involved somewhere."

"Why wouldn't they mention that? Did you know anything about this?"

John leaned back and laughed. "Cuz they're big New York City smart guys! You're from New York, you know how it is. People like that find a way to take every penny they can. And they drew up the contract, right? So, they can hide whatever they want. They might be rich already but if people like that can line their pockets some more, they will. That's how business works these days."

Simon considered John's logic.

"And how in the hell could I have known about any of this anyway?" John continued. "You volunteered us for this shit – and we're grateful of course. But big business guys like that are all about 'more, more, more.'"

Simon looked down at his boots, willing them to kick his own ass for his naivete. John leaned forward, scanning the register that sat open on the desk. "You know, this feels like the collection plate in church. They might tell the congregation what it's for, but you just know the priests and nuns and whoever else are getting a take." Simon shot an angry glance at his cynical friend.

"I didn't mean – "

Simon waved him off. "I always wondered that too, but *I* never – "

"Is that why you left the priesthood?"

"Not entirely," Simon said. "I admit there seemed to be some greed and control in the parish that I didn't agree with – probably happens everywhere. I was only ordained for a few months anyway. Just long enough to get suspicious about certain things. And I couldn't put up with celibacy."

John smiled and nodded his understanding.

"I wanted a family. Knew it when I first set eyes on Vivian. We married, had a son. And then – "

"When's the last time you've seen either one of them?"

"Not since before I came here. She wanted the big city but ended up moving to some hick town near Chicago. I wanted the peace and quiet of the country. She blamed the bottle; I blamed the bank. Ended it almost as soon as it started."

Simon stared forlornly at the ground.

"Which do you regret more? Losing your family or the Church?" The question came out a bit blunter than John intended.

Simon opened a desk drawer and retrieved a half drunk bottle of whiskey. "What's the difference? They are both families; except one can exist without the other. Church has been easier to deal with. No ties left there. In truth, the parish is probably glad I left before I ruffled their feathers too much. Hell, I got out at the right time. Just as I was leaving, some investigator showed up, claiming to be from the Vatican. Only met him once. He was asking if I'd seen a certain man around the church or heard about any strange books or valuable objects gone missing. But that wasn't even the strangest part. He looked...different."

John leaned back in his chair. "Different?" he asked.

"It was the way he kept staring at me, like he was waiting for me to reveal something. Or...or that he knew me somehow. I ignored him as best I could since I knew I was leaving. But I never forgot his face. Brightest blue eyes you ever saw, like they were lights or something. Long dark hair. Looked young but weathered, like he'd just walked a thousand miles. And so serious looking. I swear he never smiled once."

He reached for the ledger. "But that was a long time ago." He turned his eyes to John and pointed at the ledger. "This is now." He stood, seizing an opportunity to change the subject. "We need to come up with something."

John nodded. "What if we just mark each coffin twice? As far as they're concerned, that's double the count, right?"

"I thought of that," Simon said, peeking through the tent to make sure nobody was within earshot. "But it's too easy for them to check. The numbers they need are in actual coffins moved. Falsifying the records won't cut it."

"So, we need to move more coffins then," John said flatly.

"Robert said the same thing. But it's not like there are that many official graves here. We can't just make new ones appear."

Simon returned to his chair and stared blankly at his desk. Then, after a few seconds' thought, his eyes shot open wide. "Or can we?"

~ * ~

A dense fog hovered near the ground on Monday morning, engulfing the rolling, green hills in an ominous haze. Simon was the first to arrive at the cemetery. He assembled a meeting with the rest of the group at the rusty gates before they started the day's work. Once all the men were there, Simon explained what he and John suspected about their lightened payments.

He slowly revealed the idea he and John came up with. When he finished, Simon looked at each of the shocked faces before him.

Simon held his arms out. "I understand if you don't want to do this. But as it is, I have unwittingly trapped us into doing extra work for far too little. It's an insult, at best. My oversight is my responsibility and I apologize. To reconcile, I am offering this one way to make the effort truly worthwhile."

Franklin, one of the nightwatchmen, raised his hand. "But how can we prove the sheer number of new graves? Won't they be suspicious?"

"Likely," Simon said. "But this graveyard goes back a long way. Not all the records are accurate. Who knows how many bodies are really buried here? So, we can say that we unearthed many old, improperly buried corpses – hell, even *parts* of corpses. All without coffins, in unmarked graves." Simon's grin grew wider as he spoke. "As such, we are now just doing our respectful duty to give them a proper burial. They won't dispute that."

"Yeah, and Frankie, that would play well for you," Paul, the other nightwatchman said. "You're fixin' to be a mortician, right? Hell, that's why you got second shift anyway – push comes to shove we could tell 'em this is part of your study or some shit." Nobody laughed.

The men were hard to read. Had Simon missed something in his idea? Had he explained it poorly? Or was it just sick? Just a sick plan that nobody in their right, moral mind would do? He looked at John, who stood off to the side, sullenly staring at the ground. He thought that this plan could work, but it sounded even more macabre now that Simon had spoken the scheme aloud.

"Look fellas, we're already moving the dead anyway. This is the only way to make it appear we are just moving *more* of them," Simon said.

The four men in front of Simon stood motionless, eyebrows raised, but they offered no outward objections. A lengthy silence filled the misty air near the cemetery's crooked gates.

Jesper nodded. So did Billy. Then they all did.

When Simon at last believed he had their acceptance, he flashed a yellow-toothed grin at John, who could only muster a short smirk. "Very well. Let's get to it."

Simon directed Billy and Jesper to the workshop to start nailing together child-size coffins. John, meanwhile, would continue to supervise the unearthing and reorganizing of the main graves, to make it appear as though their work continued as usual. Three of the smaller coffins were ready by mid-morning, as the six of them gathered around the freshly unearthed casket of one Marjorie Tiller, wife of James J. Tiller, founder of Tiller Bank & Trust. Simon nodded toward Billy and Jesper.

With hammers and crowbars, they set to work on prying the coffin lid ajar. Everyone gathered around as they removed the wooden covering. Inside lay a woman in an expensive-looking blue dress. She was clutching a black silk bag. A silver necklace rested just below her jaw and her left ring finger bore a bejeweled, golden band. Upon seeing the apparently wealthy woman inside, each of the men got the same idea. Even if the silk pouch contained nothing of monetary value, the jewelry this woman wore alone would be worth more than their combined payout on this project.

Simon wiped the back of his sun-drenched neck with a dirty handkerchief. His heart raced as he stepped toward the body of Mrs. Tiller. He breathed deeply, wincing at the pungent stench of stale earth and bodily decay. He reached in slowly, and carefully pried the silk bag out of the corpse's near-skeletal hands.

A thin smile broke on his face when the bag chinked.

Soon every object buried with Mrs. Tiller had been removed. Ear-to-ear grins abound everyone in the group, all sharing the same unspoken realization of instant wealth that moved them to an animated excitement.

"Not a word of this to anyone," Simon ordered. "We'll divvy up the findings between the six of us, one coffin at a time. Now, let's get this here Tiller lady quartered and into the small boxes. Then on to the next."

~ * ~

The crew continued the dastardly work as the weeks wore on. Not every unearthed grave held private treasures, but enough of them did to exponentially increase each man's wealth.

One evening after work, Simon limped to his tent-office, leaned his muddy pickaxe against the desk and collapsed into his chair. He puffed on another cigar and sipped from a bottle of what he considered no longer expensive whiskey. He read and reread his updated ledger by lanternlight with a wicked grin splitting his rugged face. His take-home pay had nearly doubled – not counting the deceitful trinkets he ransacked from the dead. Images of fine tailored suits and sprawling estates filled his mind as John walked in.

"How's it looking?" John asked, his newfound golden necklace gleaming in the lantern's dull yellow light.

Simon's smile gave him his answer. "They're not wise to anything. Even Robert thinks he's partly responsible for the pay increase, being a smart business wannabe and all. I told him we struck gold-in-dead. The only thing Wyndish & Redding care about is finishing the move by the end of the summer, they don't care how," Simon said, getting an encouraging nod from John. "They just want the area cleared so they can start laying tracks before the snow sets in. They haven't even asked about all the new plots we've dug up."

"They bought the unmarked graves story?" John asked, his voice high with excitement.

"I told them we had to move all of them too before one of their workers starts hammering railroad tracks right into skulls and such."

John pulled up a chair, as a wicked grin spread across his stubbly face. "Perfect!"

"*Almost* perfect," Simon corrected him before taking a swig from his bottle. "We ain't outa the woods yet. Just need to be mindful."

John rubbed the back of his neck. "Of what? They haven't caught on, we're getting rich, the job is getting done. Everybody's making out good on this one!"

Simon admitted John had a point. He stared at him as he rolled a scripted bronze ring around in his unclean fingers. A sparkling blue sapphire was set in the middle. It looked old; could've been someone's family heirloom. After a long pause, Simon spoke up. "You ever wonder if this is all right?"

"Ah, that's just the old priest in you asking that," John waved at the air. "We're taking our fair cut is all. Besides, the railroad boys must be happy with our work, and it wouldn't be the worst thing to get on their good side, if you know what I mean? With the iron mines up north and all the railways connecting around here, something big is happening. Word is Rockefeller and

Carnegie are working on the bankroll. And with the election coming up, we could be on the ground floor of making some real big bucks."

Simon nodded absently. He heard his friend, but wasn't listening, a pang of guilt still hovered like a swarm of summer gnats – harmless but annoying.

"Tell me Father," John joked, "Did we kill these people? No. And their stuff? Hell, they can't take it with them. Better left to folk who can use it here on Earth."

John could really annoy Simon at times, but in reality, he was a shred wiser than he led on.

"Still got to be careful," Simon said. "Nobody is clean in this. Not just the legal stuff either." He let out a slow sigh. "I'd be lying if I said something didn't feel kind of wrong about it. Former priest or not. Even angels are in Hell, John."

Simon looked back at the ring, setting off another lengthy quiet.

"It's almost as pretty as mine!" John said gleefully, breaking the silence. When Simon looked up at him, John tapped the golden pendant around his neck with the faded emerald ring on his right index finger.

Simon chuckled and offered the bottle to John, who gulped down a mouthful, slowly exhaling its smooth, oaken aftereffects as if in celebration. He looked at the expensive bottle like he was proud to drink from it. Just as he stood to leave, a *snap,* like the breaking of a thick branch outside near the tent interrupted their mirth. Simon and John froze and stared at one another.

A crunch of the leaves. Another. And another. Then a low, guttural wheeze came from just beyond the entrance flap – like a weak, *sick* attempt at a howl. The sound broke into a growl, rising in volume as it morphed into a shrill screech – a noise unlike anything a dog could make. It sounded like it came from something big. Something wrong.

"Wolf?" John mouthed silently to Simon who only shrugged. There were wolves roaming the hills in this area, but none ever sounded like that. Simon reached for the pickaxe. He looked to the tent's entrance, expecting some monstrous creature to bound right in on them.

The screeching stopped. The tease of slow footsteps inched across the parched summer earth. Then...nothing. All was silent for a beat. John started to stand, slowly, just as the footfalls outside kicked up in a scurry and then trailed off. The two men exhaled.

"Maybe it was. Something was wrong with it though, making a sound like that," Simon said, pointing to the bottle. "Or it might've smelled this five dollar whiskey!" They resumed laughing proudly.

John peeked cautiously through the tent flap and looked around. "Nothing there now," he said, and threw an absent wave at his boss. "See you

20

tomorrow," he called over his shoulder. Simon returned his attention to the ring, relaxing with both feet up on his desk.

~ * ~

The next morning, the crew reported for work at the usual time. Almost everyone.

By noon when John still hadn't arrived, Simon feared he wasn't just oversleeping. He hustled to the near-derelict wooden cabin that John had been leasing and ran up the porch to the front door. It was locked. Repeated knocks went unanswered. He stepped through the weed-infested property around to the back, finding that door locked as well. He peered through the dingy windows as best he could only saw parts of the rooms inside. Simon hopped back up on the porch and gave one more fruitless rap on the front door, but when he turned to leave, he noticed strange marks along the bottom two porch steps. Carved into the wooden stair treads were a series of rough gouges, as though hewn through with a dull blade. The marks went deep into the wood and were so fresh he could smell the pine beneath the petrified surface. The scratches led off the steps and trailed out into the muddy yard for a few feet before disappearing completely.

Simon circled the cabin once more, but John was nowhere to be found.

There weren't many places for someone to go in a one store, one tavern town like Swan River. Lost in thought, Simon trudged back across town to the graveyard. As he made his way down the fence-lined gravel road along the edge of John's property, something in the roadbed glinted in the summer sunlight. He bent to pick it up but let go immediately when he recognized the familiar gold necklace. Simon suspected there were eyes on him. He looked around in all directions. Was someone playing a prank? Beads of sweat trickled down his back. He snatched up the jewelry and stuffed it in the pocket of his coveralls as quickly as he could, as if he were afraid to touch it. Then he ran down the road toward the graveyard.

The crew gaped at him in wide-eyed silence when he stumbled through the gate, drenched in sweat. He babbled in a shaky voice that John had disappeared.

"Aw shit, Simon," Jesper laughed. "He's just sleepin' off that good whiskey y'all been drinkin!"

"Yeah, boss," Billy said. "He'll turn up. Gettin's been too good not to!"

The men went back to their duties for the day.

Simon woke early the next morning after a restless night and made his way to the cemetery. As he fumbled with the gate lock in the pre-dawn light, two men stepped out from the shadows behind the gate post.

"Simon Granville?" the taller of the two men asked. They wore identical tailored suits, appearing black or dark gray in the low light, with matching, crested helmets. Local sheriffs.

Simon removed his own threadbare cap. "Yes, sirs, how can I help you?"

"I'm Sheriff Geoff Ragland, this is Sheriff Thomas Burrows." The other man nodded at Simon. "Sir, we'd like you to come with us now."

Simon stepped back. "Where? What is this about?"

"John Lowenthall works for you right?" Sheriff Burrows asked.

"Yes, he does. He didn't show up for work yesterday. Couldn't find him anywhere. Do you know what's happened?"

The two sheriffs looked at one another, mouths open as if deciding who should speak first. Ragland did. "You should come with us now, Mr. Granville. There's something you need to see."

Simon turned back to the gate and opened the lock. Ragland and Burrows exchanged confused looks.

"So my men can start their work."

He walked with the two sheriffs all the way to the far edge of town. By now the sun had fully risen. It was a perfect, bright morning. They led Simon to where Main Street curved out toward the hilly range, alongside the rocky shallows of the Swan River.

Burrows pointed to the river. "Over there. Our deputies have been waiting while we went to get you."

Simon followed his direction and saw three other men standing in the river, talking with each other. In front of them, something stuck out among the rocks.

The three men carefully stepped down the bank and out into the water. Simon waded through the water in between Ragland and Burrows. The cold, knee-deep water felt good against his hot skin. The bottom was as rocky and uneven as the large stones protruding from the surface.

As Simon approached, the three deputies stepped aside. Simon was struck still by the sight. He fought a wave of nausea and wavered, catching himself on one of the rocks. John's body rested half submerged in the murky water, propped up against a boulder. His eyes were fixed open, wide with fright.

Simon stood straight. "Oh shit. Shit, oh my God. John, no!"

"Mr. Moreno from the general store found him," Ragland said. "He was doing some late night fishing. Burst into our office just past three o'clock,

22

roused the deputy on duty. They got us up here right after that. Any idea what your friend John would've been doing out this way late at night?"

Simon had no answer. Everything was perfectly normal with John during their last conversation.

"I can't think of anything. We finished up work, left to go home, he just never showed up the next day."

"We searched him," Burrows said. "Nothing on him but those frayed clothes. And this." He handed Simon a careworn emerald ring. "It was under his tongue."

Simon sat on a rock; his feet still submerged in the stream. He'd gone pale. He cupped his face in his hands.

Sheriff Ragland put a hand on his shoulder. "We have to make it official, Mr. Granville. This is John Lowenthall, yes?"

Simon nodded. "I have to go tell the rest of my crew. Am I needed for anything else here?"

The sheriffs shook their heads. Simon stood and waded back out of the river toward the road.

When Simon returned to the cemetery, he saw Paul walking toward the shed. The two men locked eyes. Paul dropped his pickaxe.

"Get everyone together," Simon told him, pointing at his tent-office.

Simon sat down as Billy, Jesper, Paul and Franklin gathered around his desk. He opened his mouth to speak but closed it and looked down at his hands.

"They found John, didn't they?" Franklin said.

Simon exhaled, relieved someone beat him to it. "In the river. Nobody knows what happened."

Jesper tossed a shovel to the ground. "Damned hell."

Franklin and Billy removed their caps.

"What now?" Paul asked.

"I don't know. Won't know until we figure out what happened, how he got down there, and why. For today, pack up. Take the rest of the day off. Come back tomorrow morning, we'll decide then."

"You know, we're almost done," Billy said. "Why don't we just – "

"Go home, boy!" Simon said. "We aren't doing shit else today. We'll talk in the morning."

The men nodded and left the tent. Simon followed and went straight for the gate.

"Lock up on your way out!" he called back.

Simon sat alone in his cabin later that night, rocking nervously in his chair. His mind raced. He raised a new bottle, offering a silent toast to John as he fearfully thought of all that had recently happened. About his last conversation with John. The strange, hulking animal noise outside the tent.

Had someone been eavesdropping? Was John murdered because of what they'd been doing? Did they leave his necklace in the road knowing I'd find it? The more he thought, the harder he slugged from the bottle. Behind him, a huge shadow crossed the room, enhanced by the wavering candlelight.

He went still as a stone, cocked an ear up and listened. Simon scanned along the wall. Then the front door. An urgent fear came over him; a desperate need to get out of his house.

He stood hurriedly, nearly knocking his chair over. But he couldn't take another step without great effort, like something was holding him back. He lashed his hands out with each lumbering footfall, struggling as he lurched to the door and flung it open, eyeing the dark expanse of his property yawning before him. He broke free and fell forward, catching himself on the rotted porch railing. The trees rustled in the heavy wind that rolled across the hills.

Suddenly, a screech rent the air. *That screech.*

Simon's pulse hammered. Rapid steps thudded toward him. He caught a glimpse of unnaturally long fingers just before they tore at his chest. And again. His knees went slack as his assailant moved too fast to clearly see. He lunged toward the house. Another dark flash. The *screeching.* Another tear at his body. The pain was sharp and unrelenting. He screamed and screamed. And then...

~ * ~

He opened his eyes to darkness.

Simon sat against a cold, craggy wall, hugging his knees to his chest. He blinked his grogginess away. As his eyes adjusted, he saw a faint, reddish glow emerge ahead of him. He started to make out the space in the dim light. Small and rocky, barely bigger than his two-room shack. He stood, fighting sharp protests from his aching back.

The attack.

He ran a hand along his chest and neck. They felt dry and woundless. Was it all just a dream? If it was, where was he now? But if it wasn't...

He held on to the cold wall as he limped through the tunnel-like pathway toward the light source. The ground slanted downward and he stumbled, catching himself against the wall. He slowed, inching his steps. The path began to zigzag in short jogs. The red light grew brighter.

Further down, the tunnel opened into a wide chasm surrounding a large body of water. All around the red glow grew more vivid, like a growing flame in a fireplace. The cavern broadened out from where he stood, fading far into a distant blackness.

As he made his way down toward the darkened pool, a slow, deep chime rang out from somewhere in the distance.

The clangs grew louder near the water's rippling edge. There, tethered by chain to a stone column along the rocky bank sat a strange boat. It was longer than any fishing boat Simon had ever seen, and too tall to see inside. There were no sails, and only one mast that looked broken halfway up its length. The side of the hull had jagged, tooth-like protrusions jutting out down its length, giving the vessel a grotesque shape in the red light. He crossed his arms tightly to his chest. The boat rocked harder in the slack now, sending hollow echoes into the chasm as it banged against the rocks. The sound shook the ground beneath his feet with heavy thuds. He covered his ears, unable to bear any more of the heavy clanging but the noise persisted. Simon followed the boat's chain up to where it latched onto a hook atop the stone column. He hurried toward it to try and release the boat from its mooring and silence the deafening noise, but the column was much too tall for him to reach. He fought back tears of frustration as he looked around the ground for something to climb on to reach the chain when he was struck still by another sight.

On the ground behind the stern of the boat were dozens of large burlap sacks, resting in misty puddles. Reddish-tinged waves gently lapped around the bags, each overflowing with jewelry, coins, and other keepsakes.
Simon bent down and began sifting through the objects. He'd seen them before.

His heart raced, then sank, the guilty realization overcoming him to the point of free-flowing tears. How could all this be here? In a panic, he rummaged faster and faster through sack after sack of the ill-gotten goods: Mrs. Tiller's coin purse, the sterling silver pocket watch he had sworn Jesper took, the golden chalice buried with Father Moran. He rummaged faster and faster, carelessly slinging one familiar treasure after another out along the shore.

He sobbed openly but slowed to a stop when he realized he couldn't hear himself.

The heavy *gongs* of the metal vessel banging against the rocks were loud and clear. So were the *swishing* of the waves and even the whispery vacuum of the cavern itself.

But Simon's own cries? The sounds of his sobs disappeared into nothing.

He stumbled along the broken ground and fell to his knees, howling in silence. Leaning forward, he scattered a handful of dark gravel like a child throwing a tantrum, clenching his jaw the moment he heard the *tapping* of the little rocks skidding across the cavern floor.

Sighing, he straightened up, and, with fists balled up tight at his sides, forced the strongest scream he could muster. His throat felt as though it would burst with hot, broken glass as the air squeezed from his lungs. His eyes filled with such pressure he expected them to burst. All of this just to hear himself. And all of it fruitless. Lonely. *What have I done?*

He scanned the cavern as far as the faint red light would allow, searching for a path, a way out, another person. Anything. *And what was that smell?* A raw stench, like wormy mud after a rainstorm, wafted toward him from somewhere out on the water.

Simon stood and squinted. *It's hot.* His tousled hair stuck to his forehead as he wiped a palmful of cold sweat from his neck. He covered his nose with both hands, still lightheaded from his soundless scream, and stepped close to the gently lapping waves – too close.

Simon leapt back as the water's pinching warmth flowed over his feet. He looked out to see the surface churning at the edge of the darkness, tossing taller, foaming crests toward the bank. He jumped back further as they crashed, hissing against the stone and cascading back out toward the depths where the water gurgled and popped ever rapidly, dotting the cavern with thick pillars of white-hot steam.

Even the stench had its own warmth now, more putrid than even the fresh moose shit in the August sun Simon had had to shovel off his property so many times. He lurched over, gagging, holding his hands instinctively tighter against his nose and mouth to keep the bile from pouring out. *What…is…this?*

Suddenly, bursts of orange and red flame shot across the gurgling liquid, spreading like wildfire – but faster, much faster – covering the surface in seconds. Simon dropped his hands and shock crossed his face at the sight of the massive expanse before him; the blaze affording him his first real view. In the fire's glow, the cavern stretched on for a distance he'd never imagined, even compared to the vast, barren hills of home. *Home. How far away am I from there?*

Simon shut his eyes tight, wishing he could keep them closed long enough that maybe when he opened them again, he'd be back in Minnesota; that all this was just some bad vision. He stood still and listened to the *whooshes* of the raging flames and popping bubbles, so much like his roaring fireplace with a pot of tea on the hearth that he could've sworn he was there.

He raised his eyes slowly, erasing his reverie of home and his mouth dropped open.

Hundreds of forms had appeared on the blazing surface. Twisted, shadowy shapes with long, spindly trails that wisped about them as they writhed about in sync, as if in a dance. The forms swirled, forming into a circle on the water as though surrounding something.

They split to either side in front of Simon, revealing another figure behind them. Simon peered through the blaze, settling his gaze on the new form, one appearing more solid. More…human.

"Oh, my God," Simon mouthed.

It desperately twisted and swayed, trying to free himself but something held him in place. An object around the figure's neck glinted in the firelight. A small, golden pendant.

John!

Simon tried to shout at him, forgetting it was useless.

He waved his arms, trying to get John's attention, unknowing what it would accomplish, but it didn't matter. Simon was just relieved to not be alone anymore. At once, shrill shrieks filled the cavern as the shapes swirled back around John. *Who are you? What do you want with him?*

Suddenly, John flung his head back, his mouth cracked open in his own silent scream. Crimson gashes lined his body as the shadowy forms shrieked louder and dove at him, swiping and tearing with impossibly long arms. They closed in on him from all sides like ants to sugar, blocking Simon's view of his friend until a burst of red liquid rose like a geyser from among the mass.

The shrieking cut off, leaving a shrill echo as the sound faded away.

Many of the dark figures shifted aside again, revealing John's ribboned body, held up by something unseen. Simon held his hands to his mouth.

No, no, no! What did you do?

Behind them, John's head hung limply on his chest. He didn't move. Not even a twitch. The remnants of his flayed and bloodied body fell limp, lowering below the shapes, under the flames, and disappeared beneath the sizzling water's surface. But an instant later, he appeared where he was before. Whole again. Awake and aware with terror-stricken eyes as the shapes presented him with new agony.

As John's body drifted below the waves a second time, the sharp, squealing shrieks grew louder. And the forms turned toward the shoreline.

No, no, no!

Simon turned away, but something held him, stronger than the force in his cabin, rendering him immobile. His feet were pinned solid, arms pulled down to his sides as if he were anchored with heavy chains. *Is there really no way out? Did my servitude to God mean nothing? Am I truly abandoned here?* To him, this predicament was far too merciless.

The shapes broke away from where they'd held John, floating over to where Simon stood alone and exposed. The spiny forms glided ever closer, effortlessly, almost gracefully. They darkened, blending into the shadows of the cavernous surroundings. The piercing screams grew louder, closer. Simon shut his eyes once more. Heavy footfalls splashed to the stony shoreline, thudding closer with each step. They were nearly upon him.

The burning light went out.

Even angels are in Hell, John.

~ * ~

115

RAF Bassingbourn, Cambridgeshire, England. October 14, 1943.

The first blue-gray hues of dawn began to slowly materialize outside the briefing room windows, bringing with it a dense autumn fog. Inside the gymnasium-like building, nearly one hundred young men sat in rickety wooden chairs, chatting amongst each other between long, nervous drags of their first cigarettes of the day. A squeal from rusty pulleys rang out and quieted the chatter as someone yanked open the wide curtain on the stage, revealing a massive map of Europe on the wall behind.

The assembly included the flight officers from each air crew – the captain, co-pilot, radio operator, bombardier, and navigator. They all stared ahead. A red string ran lengthwise across the map. It started at a green star, indicating Bassingbourn, home of the Eighth Air Force's 91st Bomb Group, and stretched far to the right – farther than they'd hoped it would.

Captain Lance McCullers sat with his officers: Lieutenant Walter Raiming, Warrant Officers Steven Mills and Dan Savoy, and Flight Officer Bobby Tucker. They took their lucky seats – second row on the aisle. After their fifth mission, McCullers gave them an unofficial order to arrive early to briefing to make sure they'd always get the same spot. Around them, the room filled up with the officers from every crew on the mission that day. McCullers pulled out his steno notebook and a pencil.

Murmurs began to break the still silence.

Colonel Johnathan Mays stepped on the stage. His eyes were bloodshot, the expression on his weathered face grim and stern. "Good morning, gentlemen." The tall, strong colonel paused, looking down at the podium. The men quieted down. Finally, he took a slow breath and re-addressed his audience. "Today's mission is a return to attack the ball bearing plants at Schweinfurt."

The air was still and thick. McCullers looked over at Raiming, his co-pilot, who only shook his head. Mills stroked his thin moustache and closed his eyes. Tucker and Savoy sat motionless and numb. In a far corner of the room, someone was vomiting in a trash can.

"Nearly 300 ships in today's bombardment wing will give us a chance to turn the tide in the war, maybe for good. Ball bearings drive their war machine. Planes, tanks, ships, all of it. That's why we're going back. With this mission's success, we can start to finish this war once and for all. Good luck."

Pale, nervous faces looked about the room. Eyes locked and heads nodded at one another both in comfort and confidence. Silently, each man sat wondering who among them would make it back. Colonel Mays backed away and pointed to another officer. Major Dan Greely, a stocky, bespectacled man on the wrong side of a few too many mess hall donuts walked up to the podium to begin the briefing.

"Okay, gentlemen. Let's listen up."

~ * ~

In the gloomy yard next to Hangar Two, Staff Sergeant Charlie Granville sat at a picnic table with the rest of the enlisted crewmen. The men had been in full flight gear since shortly after being rattled out of their bunks in the predawn darkness.

The yards at the base always looked different when they were awaiting their officers return from briefing, Charlie thought. Much less vibrant than on days off when they'd play football or baseball, or just lounge around with the fellas, telling oft-embellished stories of their families and personal interests back home.

"Your crew is your brotherhood, kid," Charlie remembered Sergeant Michael "Mickey" Mouser saying to him when he first arrived on base, just before Mickey took off on a mission somewhere over Europe. And a brotherhood they became, Charlie realized. Being trapped in a frozen tank flying at 30,000 feet while being shot at from all directions for hours on end, they had to be. Wherever they were going, they'd face the dangers as a single unit. Looking at his fellow crew now – his brothers – after all they'd been through, he wanted to tell Mickey he was right. And to thank him for the important advice. But Mickey never came back that day.

The round-faced waist gunner stared out at the long line of B-17 Flying Fortresses parked on the tarmac, their ground crews methodically tending to each one. His home in suburban Chicago felt so far away. It'd be beautiful there, he thought, with all the oranges, yellows, and reds of autumn in their full, illustrious decay. The New York Yankees just won another World Series the other day, smashing the St. Louis Cardinals in five games. He couldn't wait to get back home and go to baseball games again. *Those damned Yanks*, he mused, still remembering the shellacking they gave his beloved Chicago Cubs back in the '38 *and* '32 Series'. He kept a framed photograph of Wrigley Field on the small table next to his cot in the Nissen hut they used as barracks that he shared with other crewmen – barracks that weren't nearly as full as when he'd first arrived. For reasons he couldn't fathom, he realized how normal that felt. How the sadness of what all those empty cots represented had become so common. He wondered if everything back home felt normal. Or safe. It was his job, half a world away, to make sure that it did – that it would be for future generations.

"The hell you staring at, Charlie?"

He wasn't surprised at the question coming from Dudley Greene, the curly-haired right waist gunner. The two worked literally side by side every mission.

"Ever notice how it's always foggy on mission days, Greenie?" Charlie said.

Sergeant Jorge Kline lit a cigarette. "It's foggy here even when it's sunny, Chuckles. What's a day in this shit without some ugly conditions?"

"Good outlook, Jorgie," Dudley said. "I think the ball is sapping your positivity."

"You spend three seconds cramped in that fucking thing and see how positive you feel!"

Dudley smacked Jorge on the shoulder. "No thanks. Lucky for us, you're the only wee lad who can fit in there."

Next to Jorge, Wally Ritter rolled his eyes and pulled a pack of smokes from under the side of his wool cap. "Give me a light, Chuckles." Charlie never liked that nickname; he only tolerated it from the boys.

"At least you fellas have some normal sense of direction up there," Wally added. "Always feels like I'm going backwards in the tail. And I rack my nuts on that little seat back there every time I fire my guns."

Standing behind them, Tommy Marini, the top turret gunner and former all-district quarterback from Akron, smiled.

"Better watch that. The wife won't like getting damaged goods back." Tommy said.

Wally shrugged. "She'll have to nurse me back to health."

Jorge hopped up and gave an exaggerated bow to Wally. "Hooray. We thank the three of you for your heroic sacrifice, fuck you very much!"

Everyone laughed.

After seventeen missions together, the ten-man crew were confident and in lockstep with one another. Eight more and they'd rotate home. Eight more and they'd be at peace. Maybe.

Their morning pep fizzled like a pinched hose when the officers approached the crew after briefing.

The enlisted men stood. "Morning, sirs!" Charlie said.

"Men, how are we this morning?" Captain McCullers asked.

Dudley nodded.

Jorge blew out a long line of smoke. "Good, Cap."

"Good to go, sir," Tommy added.

Savoy ran a hand through his wavy, auburn hair and motioned to Jorge for a cigarette with the other. Jorge tossed him his pack.

Raiming and Mills traded nervous looks.

McCullers zipped up his quilted leather jacket. "We're going back to Schweinfurt."

The crew stood still. Breathless.

"Fuck me, sir, is this a cruel joke?" Dudley said.

"Secure that shit, sergeant," Tucker snapped.

"Sorry, Tuck, but – "

"Quiet down," McCullers said. He scanned the worried faces of his crew. "Not good news, I know, boys. Higher ups think we can really turn this thing our way today, and I believe them. The target is critical."

"How many of us?" Tommy asked.

"Twenty-two from here. About 300 for the full force."

"And about 500 anti-aircraft guns and at least that many fighters," Jorge added.

Savoy and Mills stared at the ground.

McCullers sighed. "Yes, we can expect maximum opposition approaching the target. Think Wilhelmshaven or Stuttgart."

"Those were a walk in the park compared to what we've all heard about the last run to Schweinfurt, sir," Wally said.

"Whatever it is we're going to deal with it head-on. We'll get in and out as fast as we can, I promise you. We're the lead group of the entire wing, so we set the pace."

"Yeah, slow and deadly," Jorge said under his breath.

"*Enough*, Jorge," Raiming said.

"Look, boys," McCullers continued. "We aren't new to this. Just stay calm and focus on your jobs. Everyone set?"

McCullers got a few nods. "Let's pucker up and do the deed."

The crew followed their captain across the fog-enshrouded tarmac. They exchanged waves with friends on other crews who were walking to their planes. From a distance, Charlie saw their beloved B-17, *Lucky Lucifer,* waiting strong and proud on its hardstand.

When they got to *Lucky*, McCullers and Raiming went to the rear of the plane to chat with Tony, the long-time ground crew manager, as the others stood near the nose.

"Okay, here we go, fellas," Savoy said.

"Yes, father," Charlie joked, even though he appreciated his navigator's devoutness.

Dudley, Wally and Tommy knelt.

Savoy pulled out a small book from his jacket pocket and opened it to a dogeared page.

"Contend, Lord, with those who contend with me; fight against those who fight against me. Take up shield and armor; arise and come to my aid."

"Amen," Charlie responded.

Each man crossed himself.

Savoy turned from where he stood and playfully tapped a spot just below *Lucky Lucifer's* nose art – a cartoon of the Devil juggling bombs and wearing a crown fitted with the winged "8", the Army Eighth Air Force insignia – before walking under the nose to his entrance hatch.

Charlie tapped the same spot twice on his way to his entrance door on the side of the plane. Dudley followed. Each man lovingly patted the same spot below the image, a little ritual they started the day they changed the plane's name from *Jolly Lucifer* to *Lucky Lucifer*, right before their first mission together.

Jorge stood alone near the nose as the others entered the plane. He stared into the red eyes of the painted Devil, just above the plane's name, scripted in bright blue, his favorite color. He held his hand on the stout metal, remembering how *Jolly's* landing gear nearly failed to lower on their first two practice flights, prompting the name change.

And how she had saved their necks every mission since.

A voice shouted from behind him. "Paint's still holding up!"

Jorge turned to see Tony staring up at the art with a proud grin.

"That's why we asked you personally to paint it. It's bulletproofed," Jorge said.

McCullers walked between them. "Let's go Jorge." He tapped the plane in their lucky spot, then hoisted himself up through the bottom hatch. Raiming followed him up.

Jorge gave a nod at the six men who made up *Lucky's* ground crew. They pumped their fists at him for encouragement as Jorge walked to the fuselage door.

Once on board, each crew member set to work at their stations. Savoy spread out his map, pencils and compass at his station in the nose. Next to him, Mills adjusted the settings on his bombsight and tightened the mount on his bombardier's seat. Mid-plane, Jorge joined Tommy in testing the directional controls and locking mechanisms of the ball turret. Everything checked out.

In the tail, Wally locked his escape hatch and swung his turrets back and forth, making sure his controls were fluid. Further forward, Tucker reseated the plugs on his radio and clicked on his mic.

"Tower, this is Army three-one-eight, requesting a radio check, over."

"Three-one-eight, roger. Loud and clear."

"Roger, tower, over and out."

At his left waist gunner station, Charlie adjusted the sighting and ammo feed on his gun. But it was just a nervous habit. His weapon always worked flawlessly. Dudley, satisfied with his own station, stacked the extra ammunition boxes near the two men for quick access.

"Crew, assume positions for takeoff," McCullers called out over the interphone.

Charlie tightened the parachute straps on his chest and under his legs and fished his thick wool gloves from his heavy leather jacket pockets.

The crew left their positions and assembled in the radio room.

In the cockpit, McCullers and Raiming watched as a green flare was launched from the control tower – the signal to start engines.

McCullers looked over at his lieutenant. "You want to take her up?"

"Sure, just be ready to help on rudder if she drags. We're heavy today."

"That's never worried you before."

"That's because if we crashed on takeoff, it would be your fault, not mine."

McCullers smiled, but it faded almost instantly. He took a deep breath and reached out his window, pointing a "one" to the mechanic on the ground.

"Turning on one."

McCullers flipped the engine starter and mesh switches.

Lucky Lucifer thudded lightly as the number one engine on the left wing cranked over and fired.

Raiming patted the top of the instrument panel. "Take care of us, baby."

One by one, all four of Lucky's turbosupercharged radial engines roared to life.

Charlie sat against the starboard wall in the radio room and closed his eyes, feeling the deck vibrations as they taxied to takeoff position.

"We're fifth in line, boys, hang tight." Raiming said over the interphone.

A second flare fired from the control tower – the signal for takeoff. The first plane in line barreled down the runway and lifted into the gray, eastern sky. Each plane was scheduled to take off in thirty second intervals.

As the seconds ticked away, Charlie wondered if their perfect streak would continue. Seventeen missions; no aborted takeoffs. If there were any mechanical issues, now would be the best time to discover them.

"Here we go, fellas," McCullers called out.

Lucky buzzed alive as McCullers and Raiming pushed the engines to takeoff power. The plane gained speed down the runway, and Charlie felt his stomach drop as the big bomber lifted into the air. Behind them, the remaining available flights from the 91st awaited their turn.

The commanders in the tower and the ground crews watched reverently as the last plane took to the sky. When the heavy drone from her engines faded away, all action on base stopped. No one spoke. A quiet breeze drifted across the still acres of Bassingbourn as if it were suddenly abandoned.

The ground crews, having worked most of the night to prep, fuel, and arm the Fortresses, were off duty. But after a moment, mechanics all across the base set to work sweeping up the tarmac and refueling their equipment trucks. *Lucky's* crew packed up their tools and stacked them to the side of their oil-stained hardstand for easy access when – if – their plane returned.

When they finished, Tony lit a cigarette and stared down at the dirty concrete.

A young enlistee approached him. "What now, sir?"

Tony took a long drag from his Chesterfield. "Same as always, kid. We wait."

"And hope," another mechanic said as he walked by.

Tony finally blew out a long trail of smoke. "And pray if you think it'll help."

~ * ~

10:07 A.M.

"There's our escort, three o'clock low!" Lieutenant Raiming called out over the plane's interphone.

Savoy clapped his hands. "Alright, they found us!"

Charlie looked out his left side fuselage port down the ice-cold metal length of his Browning .50 caliber machine gun, as a group of P-47 Thunderbolt fighters buzzed alongside the massive bomber formation.

The weather all the way across the sea was foggy with poor visibility. Several bombers had to turn back after becoming lost in the thick clouds and wasting precious gallons of fuel trying to form up with the others. Seeing the medium-sized fighter formation confirmed that some of their escort group had been forced to do the same. But enough of them arrived, that's what mattered. They could keep the German fighters occupied, at least until their small fuel tanks ran dry.

Charlie slid his sleeve up to check his watch. Nearly three hours into the flight, *Lucky* and the rest of the lumbering formation had crossed the Belgian coastline. AFN wasn't coming through today, Charlie realized. He'd hoped Tuck was trying to find it out there on the airwaves somehow. He loved the new radio network – all the boys did. Charlie felt it was something of a link to home. *AFN would be really nice right now*. It's the perfect time, in this buffer of calm, for some Duke Ellington or Glen Miller. Charlie began humming "Easy Does It" to himself, a Count Basie favorite amongst the boys. Hard to get that number out of his head, even with the deafening noise of the plane surrounding him.

Charlie turned to Dudley but paused. Dudley stood perfectly still, head tilted, nearly leaning out of his gun port as if listening to something. He knew better than to interrupt his friend when he was concentrating. So, he turned back to his own gun port. Squinting, he peered down through the wispy cloud breaks, glimpsing sections of green and brown fields crisscrossed by rivers and roads like a patchwork quilt of the earth. He'd never really paused to take in this unique vantage point. How he longed to be safely down there, somewhere, in warmth and safety. They all did. Even the enemy. The land sure looked beautiful – and peaceful – from this height. Their handshake could wait a few more moments.

Suddenly, the hum of their escort fighters' engines buzzed up as the single-seat planes sped ahead of the bombers. The German fighters had arrived to meet them earlier than anticipated.

Captain McCullers spoke into the interphone. "Men, eyes up. Jerry's out there. Make sure everyone has their chutes on. Call everything out but keep the chatter to a minimum. It's time."

At each station, the men doublechecked their ammo load and switched off the safeties on their guns with a sharp *click*. Charlie cocked his gun's hammer to firing position and rested his frigid, gloved fingers on the triggers. No one spoke as the crew scanned the bright skies. Some miles ahead, bursts of gunfire echoed through the sky, breaking above the heavy drone of *Lucky's* engines. McCullers and Raiming watched ahead of them as smoke trails and bright flashes of the sun glinting off the fighters' canopies filled the sky. Below in the nose, Mills and Savoy stood ready at their guns, trying to discern fighter friend from foe as they closed the distance.

"Oh Jesus, there's a lot of them," Raiming said.

"C'mon little friends, tear 'em up!" someone shouted on the interphone, it sounded like Tuck.

Charlie cleared his throat againt the acrid smells of gunpowder and hot metal in the icy air. He tried to slow his breathing and not spit into his mask or risk ice clogging the oxygen tube. He hated being in a battle but waiting – listening – on the edge of it was worse.

"Left waist to bombardier, what do you see, Millsy? Talk to us back here."

"It's soup, Chuckles."

The lead bomber formation drew closer to the fray. Charlie heard smaller engines with shifting RPMs whirring and screaming against shrill machine gun fire.

"Hold your fire until Jerry is in range!" said McCullers.

"Bandits! Twelve o'clock level! Closing fast!" Savoy shouted.

"Another one high, breaking low right at us!" Tommy added.

"109s at the lead group!" McCullers called out. "Here they come!"

The German fighters surrounded *Lucky's* squadron, launching blasts of gunfire from every angle. Each ship fired back mercilessly. *Lucky* shook with the singing of her guns amidship, as empty shell casings rapidly piled up on the deck between Charlie and Dudley.

Metallic *pops* rang out among the gunfire as the air battle intensified. Thin dark lines trailed across the sky in curved, spiraling patterns.

The fighters cleared the port side, leaving Charlie to search for another target.

"*Goodnight Jane* is hit!" Raiming called out. "She's on fire, starboard side."

Charlie turned and stepped next to Dudley, looking out his gun port to their wingman, her number three and four engines engulfed in flame. She listed dangerously to her left.

"Come on guys, get out!" Charlie yelled.

Goodnight Jane pitched straight down, losing altitude rapidly. One of her crewmen bailed out from underneath her. Then another. She tumbled slowly over until she hung upside down, the fire engulfing most of the plane as she disappeared down into the clouds.

"Any chutes from *Jane*?" McCullers called.

"Thought I saw three, Cap," Dudley responded.

Charlie stepped back to his gun. He tightened his parachute straps.

Lucky flew up to the middle slot of the third element in her squadron's combat box taking up the place from the fallen *Jane*. The Luftwaffe pilots were coming in close range to the formation. Charlie's feet rattled violently on the deck as bullets struck her left side.

"Call out those fighters!" said Raiming.

"Navigator to pilot, second turn approaching. We're following the lead, sir."

"Roger, navigator. Turning with the lead ship."

The skies over Belgium resembled swarms of gnats at a campfire. Streams of gray smoke billowed in all directions.

Wally opened his mic in the tail. "Bandits, six o'clock low, coming back around!"

"I'm on 'em!" Jorge responded from the ball turret, sending a hail of bullets at the skittering Messerschmitt Bf-109s. Each Fortress pilot worked to keep their big planes in tight formation for as long as possible, despite the fighter swarm.

"Where the hell are the little friends?" McCullers called out.

Tommy responded. "First wave scattered 'em, Cap. They're strung out."

"Half-roll to starboard!"

Charlie put the rolling 109 just behind his crosshairs and squeezed the triggers. A puff of smoke shot from under the fighter as a loud *bang* sounded just to their right.

"What was that?" McCullers shouted. "Any 110s up here?"

Charlie lowered his gun barrel and watched in horror as their right wingman, *Midnight Dynamite's* left wing disintegrated.

"*Midnight Dynamite* is hit!" Charlie called. "She's going down!"

The unfortunate bomber spun completely around from the impact and quickly fell at a steep angle. Too steep.

"No chutes from *Midnight*." Tuck reported.

"Confirmed," Charlie said.

The American bomber force continued to press inland. Charlie maintained his firing barrage from the left side of the plane, throwing short, controlled bursts at incoming enemy fighters. They were everywhere. Three new basketball-sized windows had formed next to his turret, courtesy of the explosive shells and deadly accuracy of Luftwaffe pilots.

Charlie's gun steamed in the thin, subzero air. He wondered how much ammo he had used up; it felt like he had been shooting nonstop. His hands cramped. His breath came in short, ragged gasps. The fighter opposition had never been this relentless. Panicked thoughts raced through his mind – and he suspected everyone else's too.

How long to target?

How long can our escort stay in this?

When are we going to die?

The intervals between gunfire widened.

"They're bugging out, 109s and 190s breaking low and away!" Wally said.

Charlie exhaled. He placed a hand on Dudley's shoulder, who turned and nodded. Tuck re-trimmed his radio dials. The whines of Luftwaffe engines faded away.

"They'll be back," Raiming said.

McCullers throttled *Lucky's* engines back just a hair. Every man on board unpuckered for a moment. Their ears popped. Gunsmoke dissipated. The sky itself seemed to exhale.

"Everyone check your stations and call in," Captain McCullers ordered. "We're on our own for now."

The remaining P-47 fighter squadrons had formed up and were drifting back toward the bomber wing. Some were issuing smoke, but the majority looked unscathed. The lead fighter wiggled his wings at the front group, signaling they had to turn back.

"Sure wish they had bigger tanks," Charlie said as he and Dudley watched their escort from the port side dive away and head westward. As Dudley turned back to his gun, Charlie saw a Thunderbolt lagging behind the others. It was belching plumes of hot smoke, wings dipped at a slight angle. As it passed westward, the sunlight revealed a canopy bathed in crimson as its pilot tried to keep up with the other fighters. He hoped their little friends slugged it to the German fighters good.

"You heard the captain, call in!" Lieutenant Raiming barked.

One by one from the navigator to the tail gunner, each man was quick to respond.

"Navigator checking in."

"Bombardier checking in."

"Radio room okay!"

"Left waist okay, some fuselage damage on the port side."

"Right waist good."

"Top turret good."

"Ball turret okay."

"Tail okay. Pretty big chunk out of the right stabilizer."

"Roger that. Mills, time to target?" McCullers asked.

"Stand by…ETA to the IP unaffected and approaching. Still on time."

"Good!" Charlie shouted. "Let's get the fuck out of here!"

"Clear the chatter, Sargeant!" McCullers called back.

Charlie re-cocked his gun and checked his oxygen feed, always keeping the metal parts at his station moving to avoid jams from the below-freezing air.

"Stay focused, boys," Captain McCullers called out over the interphone. "Coming up on the IP."

Everyone resumed scanning the skies. Charlie's heart thudded in his chest, waiting for another wave of fighters to burst from the clouds. *Lucky's* engines maintained a steady hum. Soon even they seemed to fade off, casting a sense of illegitimate silence in the sky.

And then it happened. A single low, dull *boom* pounded the air somewhere out there.

Then another.

And another.

And then a *lot* more.

Black plumes of exploding cannon shells dotted the sky in all directions.

McCullers and Raiming scanned the skies. "We're loose," Raiming said. "A lot of stragglers out there. We're too thin!"

McCullers nodded. "Group will tighten at the IP. Flak jackets and safety straps, now!"

On *Lucky's* left, Charlie heard several ships throttle up to compensate and maintain their spot in formation. This was doubly dangerous, he realized. The high RPM's tax the good engines and also consume more fuel.

"Wonder how many are left. Anyone got a good count?" Dudley asked.

"We're taking it on the chin from what I can see," Jorge said.

Worse, every man could see the flak from the anti-aircraft guns were set to the right altitude, metallic *bangs* and *pops* sounding all around them.

McCullers looked out on either side of his own plane. *Lucky's* flight element – her and her two new wingmen – *Reich's Wreckers* and *Water Valley Warrior,* were inching closer, tightening up their formation. The IP was getting close.

In the waist, Charlie felt a pang of worry when he saw *Warrior's* third engine take a direct hit, rocking the plane violently.

"*Water Valley's* hit! Right side!" Charlie reported.

Smoke and oil belched from her wing in thick salvos but somehow, she stayed at level flight.

"Captain," Tucker said. "Squad leader over C-channel requesting to tighten."

"Way ahead of them," McCullers responded.

Throughout the plane *Lucky's* gunners braced themselves as the sky continued to erupt. The plane bobbed and swayed in quick jolts. Charlie reached down for another ammo box just as a wide, burning gash tore up through the bottom of the plane between him and Dudley, knocking them both off their nearly frozen feet.

"Underside hit! We got a nice hole in the deck," Dudley called.

"How bad?" McCullers asked.

Charlie and Dudley studied the damage. It wasn't too bad. Missed anything critical. "Waist okay, Cap," Dudley said. He smacked Charlie on the arm. "Holy shit, close one, eh?" Charlie couldn't quite tell, but he felt sure Dudley was grinning behind his oxygen mask. He wasn't sure if Dudley was talking about the flak nearly hitting them, or the fully loaded bomb bay just a few feet away.

Every thud lifted their boots off the deck. Shell casings bounced all around the tight space like pebbles in a can. Directly under their plane, tucked tightly in the ball turret, Jorge had a spectacular, if terrifying view of the AA defense far below. It started as hundreds of tiny white sparks on the surface and exploded all around them as deadly, concussive bursts seconds later.

Entering the IP through to delivery was the worst part of each mission, Charlie thought. At least fighters gave you something to shoot back at. With flak, you just had to hope to make it through. And you were vulnerable. Deathly exposed, like running blindfolded through a minefield. Adding to the helpless fright was that Captain McCullers couldn't maneuver too much one direction or another to avoid the barrage. They had to fly directly through it in order to stay on target and on time. It always felt like it took much longer than it should. "We're at the IP. Closing in," Captain McCullers called out over the interphone. He flipped the flight controls down to the bomb sight in the nose. "Switching over now. She's all yours, Millsy."

Below the cockpit, forward in the nose, Mills was "flying" the plane. The flak field grew thicker and heavier the closer the attack force got to the target. Every crew on every Fortress longed for the bombs to drop.

"Bandits! Five o'clock low!" The interphone callout had to be a mistake.

"What? With all this flak? Check and re-confirm!" Charlie shouted back as he scanned the skies on his side.

"Confirmed! Confirmed God damnit!" Jorge screamed immediately as a shower of bullets pelted the underside of the right wing. Waves of German 109 and Focke-Wulf 190 fighters snuck in and jumped the formation at high speed from behind and below, flying right through their own anti-aircraft assault. Guns from the fighters and bombers blazed in all directions.

"Time to target? Give me a number!" McCullers ordered.

Suddenly, a violent hail of Luftwaffe bullets shattered the right corner of the Perspex windshield and cockpit instrument panel. McCullers screamed as plexiglass and metal shrapnel showered him and Lieutenant Raiming.

The interphone crackled. "Bomb bay doors open! Stand by! ETA to target, one minute," the bombardier called out.

"One minute confirmed," Savoy said, setting his stopwatch down and sketching a pencil line on his map.

Three 190s drifted up right alongside *Lucky Lucifer*, mere yards from Charlie's side. He held his fingers on the triggers, unleashing sizzling .50 caliber rounds right at them. A big smoke stream issued from the underside of the trailing fighter. It turned over, burning, and fell to the earth.

"Target ahead!" Mills said. We're on point, visibility less than optimal."

"Fucking of course it is! Always clear until we get to the target. Hang on, fellas. Ten seconds," Savoy said.

"Roger," McCullers grunted. Even through the crackling interphone he sounded like he was speaking through gritted teeth. Blood covered most of his right side. He hoped the lead bomber, on whose command the entire group will release their payloads, had a better view of the target. They couldn't even think of going around again for a second attempt. To his right, Raiming lay lifelessly pinned against his right side window, a river of blood cascading from the plexiglass shards wedged in his forehead and throat.

Given the damage, McCullers expected their ship to feel heavy once he resumed control. He gripped the controls tightly and keyed his mic. His breath came in short gasps. "We…we have one shot at this. Only one. Do you copy Mills?"

"Roger. Almost there, watching the lead ship."

After her squadron reshuffled following the first attack, *Lucky* was in the number five position, a clear view of the lead combat box just ahead. The seconds before delivery were always long, but this felt like a new kind of unending agony.

In the waist, Charlie was still scanning the skies for nearby enemy fighters. Most were too far aft of his position, pestering the ships in the rear of the formation. *Come on Millsy, drop the fuckers!*

"Bombs away!" Mills announced over the interphone.

The Fortress shuddered as the hefty cluster of bombs released from her belly. "All bombs out! Switching control to cockpit. Closing bomb bay doors. She's all yours, Cap," Mills said.

No reply came from the captain as he regained the sluggish controls.

Moments later, a trail of primary and secondary explosions dotted the land far below as giant pillars of dark gray smoke covered the area for miles. *We hit it! We had to have hit it*, Charlie thought.

"Please get us out of here!" shouted Wally over the staticky interphone from his gunner's position in the tail.

In the cockpit, Captain McCullers, weak and bleeding from wounds that seemed to be everywhere, blinked away the pain. He banked the big plane hard right and whined her engines up to nearly full throttle.

Charlie stared out his gunport as the captain executed the turn. The angle afforded him the ghastly view of many other bombers burning in the sky, though still turning for home. The remainder of the force was scattered across the area. Charlie lowered his eyes, knowing there were holes for the German fighters to punch through.

Just then, a group of 109s approached fast from astern. Charlie resumed his defensive fire, with Dudley covering their other side.

"Half roll from 4 o'clock, nail 'em Greenie!" Tommy shouted.

A violent thud rocked the cramped waist room, knocking Charlie forward against his gun. Bright sunlight and bitter cold flowed into the room. He turned to see a gaping hole in the starboard fuselage. Right at Dudley's gun.

Charlie squeezed his mask to clear some of the slush that had formed inside. "Dudley's hit! He's…gone! Right waist is torn apart!"

"Left waist, are you – "McCullers started to say.

Boom.

He alerted the crew to a new problem. "Number four!"

Smoke billowed out of *Lucky's* number four engine and trailed in through the cracked fuselage, filling Charlie's compartment with dense, oily smog. The plane listed lazily to the left. Charlie felt his stomach drop as the plane suddenly dipped altitude and he heard the engines throttle back as the captain feathered the number four prop. *Shit, we're going to straggle*, he realized. The worst place for a bomber to be. Out of formation. Unprotected. If they were unable to keep up with the others, enemy fighters would swarm them like sharks to a whale carcass.

Charlie expected the bailout bell to ring any second, but no such sound came. He pulled himself up, staggered back toward his gun, dazed and cold. Another heavy burst rattled the plane amidship, knocking him back to the deck. He heard the engines throttling up and down, trying to find the right compensation for one another. Smoke continued to fill the waist section.

Wally called over the radio from the tail. "Bandit! pulling through 10 o'clock low. He's all yours, Charlie!" The last thing Charlie saw was his own gun as he tried to cock the frigid hammer back to firing position.

~ * ~

The dull drone of the engines sounded far away and faint, like the ambiance of a dreamy doze on a long train ride. Charlie tried to blink but could only slightly open one eye. Beams of light streamed through the shredded midsection of his plane. His head throbbed sharply. A thick bandage, caked with something cold and slushy felt like a helmet on the left side of his head. A hand patted his chest reassuringly. "Lie still. We're going home." It was Flight Officer Tucker, the radioman. His hands and flight suit were splattered with blood and oil.

Charlie whispered. "How bad?"

Tucker shook his head.

Charlie coughed. "How bad, Tuck?"

"McCullers, Raiming, and Dudley are gone. You and Mills are banged up pretty bad."

"McCullers *and* Raiming? Then who's…?"

"Savoy has her. He's been hit too."

Tommy patted Charlie's shoulders. "The rest of the boys are right here, Chuckles."

"Thank God he had some flight training," Wally said of their navigator.

Tucker looked about the bloody, pulverized cabin. He didn't know how long the plane could hold out. They were clear of enemy territory. They had made it back somewhere over the North Sea, but they had to be dangerously low on fuel. Charlie had the same thought. The fear of having to ditch in the frigid water made his heart thump anew. One third of the crew was already dead. Others had serious wounds. Charlie stared at the floor as frightful thoughts raced through his mind. It was doubtful they could survive a crash landing. If they had to put her down in the sea, would anyone rescue them? Fighter escort usually picked up the bomber force on their way back, but if nobody saw them or knew they were still flying...

Reaching their base seemed improbable, if not impossible. If they could get back over England, they could try to set her down in one of the soft, endless fields, but in the plane's condition...

Charlie's eyes felt heavy, and the light dimmed as they skimmed the sea. In the cockpit, the injured navigator struggled to keep their battered bird in the air.

"Hey, who is – ", Charlie stammered, pointing toward the front of the plane. The surviving crew looked but only saw the scorched interior of their stalwart bomber.

"Just lie still, buddy," Jorge said, reassuringly.

Long minutes passed. Tommy nodded at Wally, who gave a thumbs up to Tucker. He smiled encouragingly at Jorge. Mills lay unconscious between them, his parachute harness cinched down as a tourniquet for his abdomen. Jorge reached over and covered Mills' hands with his own. Until that moment, nobody had noticed their stricken plane seemed to be flying smoother and straighter than before.

"How long now, Tuck?" Charlie asked.

"Not much farther, just hang on," Tuck said. "I'll be right back."

The interphone was completely shot out. Tucker stood in the cramped space and limped on a tourniquet-wrapped leg forward toward the cockpit, shouting for Savoy. Clearing the radio room, where the bodies of his three fallen crewmates lay, he inched across the narrow catwalk in the empty bomb bay and looked up into the cockpit. Savoy sat slumped forward, hanging in his seatbelts. He couldn't believe his eyes when he saw a man with long, flowing silver hair in the other seat. Tucker immediately limped back to rouse the others as a blinding white light enveloped his view.

From his position further aft, Charlie and the other men ducked away from the bright glow. At first, he thought it was the late afternoon sunlight glinting perfectly off the waves below, but they were now flying over land.

The saturation was intense, like no other light he had ever seen. He finally snapped his eyes shut and began to pray.

Moments later, a jolting thud snapped him from unconsciousness.

Empty shells, flak shrapnel and battle debris rattled through the interior of the plane as the broken hulk slid across pavement and muddy earth. The gaping hole in the right side of the fuselage widened, nearly tearing the plane in two. Only the taut steel cables inside the aircraft's sturdy frame held it together. The smoldering wreck plowed ahead until what was left of her plexiglass nose dug violently into the damp earth, throwing the surviving crew forward with a blunt force as the plane finally came to a twisted stop.

They had made it.

Charlie lay back, dazed, another broken component among the charred, bloody remains of their beloved plane. That's when it all came rushing back to him, the hell they'd just been through. Almost half his crew – his brothers – were dead. Many other friends he knew just that morning were killed or missing. He had no idea how badly he was hurt or even if he'd survive much longer. And he didn't care. Tears came uncontrollably; some for gratefulness. Some for fear. Most for sorrow.

Sirens and shouting voices of emergency crews approached. The *shooshes* of fire extinguishers shot out everywhere. A different chaotic cacophony than what he'd heard all day.

"Sir? Sir? Stay still, we've got you!" someone yelled into the cabin.

"Medic! Medic!" another shouted.

"Over here!"

Charlie couldn't tell if the voices were in panic or relief. "Take it easy gentlemen, help is here, you're okay!"

"Oh, Jesus Christ, you poor bastards."

Charlie could not fight the total exhaustion that overcame him, and he lost consciousness for the last time.

~ * ~

Thick warmth flowed over him from somewhere nearby.

Charlie cracked open an eye. Closed it immediately. He lay in a bed, listening to the soft whir of a fan – or it could have been the stove heater. There were distant voices. And footsteps. Lots of footsteps. Painfully, he forced open his unbandaged eye, his vision blurred against the bright light of the room. His whole body felt cold despite the radiant heat near the bed. Everything hurt.

"Just a few minutes, if you can manage," someone said from across the room. "He's going to be in and out for a while yet."

"Understood."

Charlie heard someone approach and set something down on the bed near his feet. "Sergeant Granville? Can you hear me? Sergeant?"

Charlie tried to respond. His throat felt like rocks. "Y – yes?"

Some of the blurriness cleared. A tall, dark haired man in full Army dress stood near his bed. "Glad to have you back, airman. Just take it easy. I'll be quick. I'm Major Briggs, with the OSS. Secret Intelligence division."

"OSS?" Charlie grimaced as he tried to sit up. "What do you want with me?"

"Relax Sergeant. You're not under investigation for a thing. I'm looking into other matters that you may have witnessed. I just have a couple questions and then I'll let you rest; bastards did a number on you up there."

"Go on, sir."

"I need you to try and tell me something. What landed your plane?"

Charlie held on to the question for a long, silent moment, unsure how to respond.

"What do you mean, *what*?"

"Pardon me. I meant, *who*. Who did you see up there?"

"I saw nothing. The boys said Savoy was at the controls. I guess he got us home."

"Is that what you believe? Or what you saw?"

Charlie closed his barely working eye. "What's the difference?"

"The difference, son, is everything," Major Briggs said. "Let me put it to you from my perspective. Two days ago, a B-17 returned from Schweinfurt with only one engine barely turning and the rest of her so badly damaged she shouldn't physically have been able to stay airborne, let alone remotely intact after what by all eyewitness accounts say wasn't the smoothest of belly landings. She's being hauled for scrap as we speak. Crushed beyond repair. On top of that, everyone on board with any amount of flight experience was already dead. I've been sent here to figure out how this impossible landing happened."

Charlie was in no mood for this, despite his own curiosity. "Call it an act of God, then, sir."

Major Briggs nodded, already convinced he'd get nothing more out of Charlie. He picked up his briefcase and moved toward the door but turned back to Charlie.

"And the Lord said to Satan, 'Whence comest thou?' And Satan answered, 'From going to and fro in the earth, and walking back and forth on it.' Job 1-7. Check it out, son. I think you'll like that one.

~ * ~

Dayton, Ohio 1995.

Thousands of people gathered near a huge hangar at Wright-Patterson Air Force Base for the gala event of the annual Dayton air show. Three B-17 Flying Fortresses and several different American fighter planes had been meticulously and perfectly restored to flying condition to commemorate the 50th anniversary of the War's end.

Steel cane in hand, Charlie Granville sat in the front row of the VIP area along with a group of other surviving pilots and aircrew for the ceremony and unveiling of the old warbirds. The hangar doors opened and each of the big Fortresses were towed out parade-style to the roar of the cheering crowd.

Memphis Belle of course was first. She always got the publicity, the fame and the movies, Charlie thought with a smile. He flew alongside her for a few missions before they rotated out. Good fellas, great bird. *Starduster* was next in line. He hadn't heard of her, but nonetheless applauded her contribution and the gorgeous restoration she now displayed. Moments later, Charlie yanked his Aviator sunglasses off and stared wide-eyed and still when he saw the all-too-familiar nose art on the next plane that rolled out onto the tarmac before him. He had no idea why – or *how* – *Lucky Lucifer* could be here. There was nothing left of her after Schweinfurt. A replica, he rationalized, or they just put her art on another plane. The crowd applauded enthusiastically. Attendees waved flags. The retired airmen and younger, active duty personnel stood and saluted.

Tucker shouted over the applause. "Can you believe it Chuckles? She looks brand new!"

Charlie's mind drifted back to the horrors of that last mission. Every day for the last 52 years, Charlie couldn't understand – couldn't *believe* – how he had survived that day. The strange interrogation with Major Briggs right afterward only added to his suspicious feelings. Even now at the celebration, his darkened thoughts brought a bland taste to his beer and an empty feeling to his gut.

He couldn't take his eyes off his old plane, this perfectly restored facsimile, resting strong and statuesque just as she had on that greasy hardstand all those years ago. The chatter of the celebration faded away, replaced in his head by echoes of ancient gunfire and screams. The roar of the engines at full power; the quiet stillness when they were shot out. He could see all the boys, too – standing with him at the nose, ready to climb aboard for another mission. Charlie snapped his wet eyes shut against the memory.

When all the old planes took their positions on the tarmac, the congregation moved back into the hangar for cocktails and music. A Glenn Miller Tribute orchestra was setting up on the big stage. Many stayed out near the planes, taking pictures and getting a rare look at victorious history up close.

"Haven't you ever wondered about that day?", Charlie asked his old friend as he came out of his stupor. "I can't hold my tongue anymore. Just tell me the truth, Tuck, finally! You saw something." He glanced around to make sure no eyes or ears were upon them. "*We* saw something."

"Charlie, you've got to let it go," Tucker said, placing a hand on his shoulder. "We made it back. We came home. Call it what you want, but I say it was just a damned good airplane – and some good luck, I'll give you that. I just wish we were all still here. But you need to stop thinking about it so much."

Charlie looked down and shook his head, unconvinced.

"Look. Anything we saw," Tucker made quotation marks with his fingers, "Was battle stress. That's it. Happens to everyone who did what we did."

When Charlie didn't acknowledge him, Tucker sighed and started to walk off, unable to bear anymore of Charlie's unappreciative sentiments. He stopped, then pulled his friend toward him in a supportive embrace. "Talk to you later, pal."

As he watched him go, Charle realized, finally, that Tucker was right. He'd led a good life since the war. He married well. Had two good children. He needed to let that mission go, for good. He stepped after Tucker, needing to have a beer with his friend and apologize for being disrespectful. But a deep, velvety smooth voice from behind held him back. "Leave him, Charles."

Charlie turned to see a tall man in a finely tailored black suit. His long, near-sterling hair was tied back, accentuating sharp features and eyes whose gold irises sparkled with a curious radiance in the brightly lit hangar. He looked immediately familiar.

"You!" Charlie nearly shouted. He suddenly remembered Mission 115 like it had just happened. Including this man's appearance in his beloved *Lucky.* "Who are you?"

A wide, proud grin spread across the man's face.

"I think you already know."

An understanding crept in as Charlie beheld the stranger before him. "I–I can't– "

"You've gained some wisdom through the years, Charles. Ever since that day, you've known, somehow, that something wasn't quite right. You've peered through the veil just a hair, where your friends haven't, am I right?

You've experienced things, though you still don't trust your intuition very well. Neither did your grandfather," the man said with a sigh. "Don't be a shortsighted speck like Simon was."

Charlie clenched his jaw.

The man looked him up and down. "You look like him, you know."

"My grandfather? I never knew him."

Charlie looked about the hangar, feeling they were being eavesdropped on. But the other attendees at the ceremony mingled about, nursing their cocktails and memories, paying no attention to him or the man.

"I made something of a deal with him long ago," the man said. "I've been waiting for the opportunity to honor his unintended devotion. When I learned you were in that little fight over there it became more than some vicarious voyeuristic empathy on my part. I sought for the chance to watch out for you."

"*Little* fight!" Charlie dropped his cane before he swung it at the man. "Those were years of hell. Millions of people died! That war changed the whole world!"

"War? Years of hell?" The stranger laughed, clapping his hands. "You've never experienced a moment of either, Charlie Boy. You don't know what war is. Millions of deaths, you say. Changing the world? That was entertainment, nothing more. And you barely played a part in *that*." He ran both hands back through his smooth ashen hair and stood slate rigid. "When you *start* a war – a real one on a scale that changes not just this world but many. When it even creates new worlds, and in the aftermath uncountable numbers of people both revere and abhor you, then you can tell me about what war *really* is. But here you are. Because of *me*. I know you don't understand. I suppose your lack of perspective matches that of your instinct."

"Jesus Christ, I – "

"Not *him*!" the stranger shouted, drawing a few curious looks from those within earshot. "*He* had nothing to do with any of it, I assure you," the man said with a flippant wave of his hand. "*I* decided to help you that day. I saved you. I'm only sorry I was too late for your friends, but I –" He jerked his head upward in rapt attention, as if scolded by an angry parent. His grin faded.

The man cut his eyes down toward Charlie. "Noble deeds also tend to get His attention."

Charlie looked out toward the tarmac, fixated at the nose art on his now-renowned B-17. "Well, why– "

But the silver-haired man was already walking away. Charlie bent down to pick up his cane as he heard the man snap his fingers playfully to the beat and whistle the familiar melody to "Easy Does It."

~*~

The Best There Ever Was

"Holy shit! Pete Mesnor! Are you kidding?" Joe stood from his desk chair.

Vinnie leaned back, kicking his feet up on his own cluttered desk. He waved the handwritten letter around, as if for proof. But mostly just to show off. "Never thought I'd get the chance to interview him, especially now at his age. But he agreed to do it. I think he was surprised I'd found him." He smiled and looked dreamily at the cracked plaster ceiling.

Joe tapped a stack of papers with his pencil. "And all I can get here are city council meetings and high school basketball. He's not still here in Pittsburgh after all this time, is he?"

"Up in Erie. Meeting him Thursday night. This is it, pal, the story I've been waiting for!"

What an understatement, Vinnie thought as he spoke. Ever since he fell in love with baseball as a kid and heard the tale of 'ol Pete Mesnor, he was hooked. When he became a sportswriter, Menor's story – the murder trial, the mystery, the intrigue – was always in the back of his mind. Including how Mesnor vanished.

He could've been dead for all anyone knew. Immediately after he was removed from baseball, every big sports reporter in every city tried to get the scoop on his side of the story. But soon after, the trail got cold. Interest waned, and Pete Mesnor became just another ghost of baseball infamy.

Still, Vinnie had a feeling that someday, somehow, he'd get to do what nobody else could. He'd get to the bottom of Mesnor's tale. Screw the editors. Screw the pitch, he told himself. He was just going to take a swing on his own – and even if it cost him his job, he'd hit it out of the park.

"What makes you so lucky? How the hell did you pull this off?"

Vinnie shrugged. "That's just it. I got lucky on this one. A lead responded,"

"Come on, cut the bullshit, Panino. Spill! This might be the biggest story our little paper ever broke! Would've been the biggest sports story for any big paper in the past fifty years."

Vinnie looked around the small, ugly office, with its smoke-stained ceilings and wood paneled walls. "Alright," he gave in reluctantly, as if wanting to protect his source. He lowered his voice to just above a whisper. "One of the Pirates' top brass guys tipped me off to where he might be — after a little wheel greasin' of course," Vinnie flashed a cocky grin. "Couldn't get a phone number, but I got an address, so, I sent him a letter," he added with a shrug. "The tip suggested he likes letters. So, I thought it was kind of weird when he wrote back with a number to call. I didn't really believe it at first. Coulda been some crank yankin' my chain. But when I called and we started chatting, I started to believe it really was the man himself."

"How?"

"The way he spoke. He answered every question I asked about certain games and cities – even specific pitches – "

Joe held up a hand. "So what? Any old fan or some crack with a copy of old newspapers could answer that stuff!"

Vinnie nodded his agreement. "It was also how he knew to expect my call." He leaned in toward Joe and whispered. "He knew John Galbreath's secretary tipped me off to him. Said so before I ever mentioned it."

"Well sonofabitch!" Joe slapped his knee. "You think he's finally going to talk about what happened?"

Vinnie nodded. "I hope so. That's the whole point of this. We didn't discuss any of that on the phone though. He's never spoken about it." He stared at the wall for a few seconds, rubbing his chin. "Yep!" Vinnie slapped his desk. "Yes, yes! He's going to talk. He has nothing to gain at this stage of his life by keeping quiet. This is the time. I just know it!"

"Which is suspicious, isn't it? I mean, if he really didn't do it, then you'd think he wouldn't be so hush-hush for all these years. That whole mess is what kept him out of the Hall of Fame."

Vinnie scribbled something on a notepad. "Guess that doesn't really matter to him. Maybe he just wanted to slip away and hoped people would forget. But you're right, I mean, being a recluse for all these years hasn't helped his image. But he sure was an amazing player. You know, this is his first interview since the acquittal 50 years ago."

Joe cocked his head at his friend. "Yes, Vincent, everyone knows that about Pete." Vinnie gritted his teeth at hearing his proper name.

"But it's crazy for sure. You called it, buddy. Shit, maybe you really are psychic after all."

Vinnie raised a finger. "*Clairvoyant.* At least that's what they're calling it. It's all new. People don't believe in psychics. Even though it's got a lot of evidence behind it. It's like when people think the Bible must be bullshit because it doesn't talk about dinosaurs or whatever. How the fuck does anyone know what the truth is? Seems like no matter if people are closed minded or a true believer, they're an expert either way, right?"

Here we go, Joe thought as Vinnie continued his rant. "I've always thought the real truth about things is somewhere in the middle. But what do I know?"

Joe looked away and shook his head. He hated it when his friend went on tangents like this. "So, you think Mesnor's truth is in the middle too? Like maybe something really did happen?"

Vinnie leaned back in his chair again, clasping both hands behind his head. "It's like those who claim they believe in evolution." Joe rolled his eyes, his attempt to bring the subject back to reality was an utter failure. "They seem to just shun everything else, and they think they know for a fact how things really are. I think that's kind of what happened with Pete."

Joe raised his eyebrows; the subject changed after all.

"They heard the same story a few times and it stuck. So, it must be true, right? I get that, but that doesn't mean it's what the facts are. But whatever. None of us know everything. Anyway, back to your point, I *did* see this coming. I knew it. I *felt* it. I can't explain it any other way. Take that for what it's worth."

~ * ~

Vinnie nearly missed the turn in from the road. Bev's Tavern was one of those semi-secluded joints found on the edge of some towns. No sign by the road, no lights over the awning. The parking lot was nearly empty when he steered his prized green Buick into a space near the entrance. *That's odd,* he thought. The place should still be buzzing with the happy hour crowd – unless there were other things to do on the southern fringe of Erie on a Thursday night. At first, it didn't even look open. Then he caught a dim glow inside.

He flipped open his antique silver pocket watch, a gift from his late grandfather. Five minutes to seven. He could make out a few people through the windows of the bar. Their silhouettes backlit by neon signs. He grabbed his steno notebook and strolled toward the double wooden doors of the establishment, smiling with anticipation. Vinnie couldn't help but gloat over what this article would mean for him. Being the first person to interview Pete Mesnor since the day he was pulled from the spotlight and into seclusion is the kind of story that wins you awards – and earns you a hefty raise. As a sportswriter, a strong story like this can secure your place among the honored greats of the profession also. Mesnor was kept from the baseball Hall of Fame. With a hit story, Vinnie Panino would punch a ticket to his own.

Suddenly, both doors burst open as though kicked from inside.

Vinnie nearly jumped out of his shoes as he dropped his notebook. "Geez Louise, mister, you about gave me a grabber!" The man looked past Vinnie, staring off into the horizon as he stumbled down the short flight of steps, finally catching the railing on his third attempt. Something fell out of his pocket. He mumbled words of some kind as he searched the ground. "Got ya!" he yelled, then held up his nearly lost cigarette in triumph.

He finally regarded Vinnie, who stared back at him with a look of amused pity.

"You, uh, you okay there, buddy?" Vinnie coughed back a laugh.

"Fuckin' lame dames, my fffre…friend," he stuttered.

Vinnie had no time for this. "Yeah, they'll cause you some problems," he said as he started to move past the drunken buffoon into the bar. The man shot out a hand and grabbed Vinnie by the elbow as he walked by.

"Hey, you got a light, pal?"

"Sure," Vinnie reached for his lighter and flicked it on for him. It took the poor fellow a few attempts to light it as he whispered something about his lady friend. Cigarette finally ablaze, he took a long drag and continued his tirade.

"I mean they aren't good for nothing!" He exhaled a long blast of carcinogens. "Except some cheap talk and a pair of attitudes. I mean how can any fella have a big time with a bad titty? Am I right, guy?"

"Right you are! Take it easy, pal." Vinnie laughed as he went inside.

Thick tobacco smoke stung his eyes as he stepped into the hazy bar. He could already feel his eyes getting bloodshot as he scanned the quiet, jazzy joint, trying to locate the man who'd presumably be Pete Mesnor. There'd been no photos of him for decades. Vinnie hoped he'd guess right, but then how many men in their eighties would be in here? Most of the tables were empty. He counted only five people seated at the bar. All middle-aged men in wrinkled suits, too busy guzzling their bottled beer and chain smoking the evening away to even acknowledge one another.

A cold beer would be great in this acrid air, but it's a special occasion, Vinnie told himself as he stepped up to the bar. "Glenlivet. Neat." The stocky, grease-haired bartender gave a quick nod and added two fingers' worth of the pricey scotch to a tumbler. "Tab me. Name's Vinnie." He took his scotch and strolled to an empty corner booth near the window. The cracked, faux leather hissed as he sat down and fished out a cigarette. A neon beer sign on the wall bathed the booth in a soft red glow. He faced the window to watch for Mesnor's arrival.

A silky piano number purred from the jukebox. Vinnie took small, savory sips of his scotch between puffs of his Pall Mall, thinking of his first question to the legendary ballplayer. Vinnie checked his watch. 7:13 PM. *He's running late. Hope he didn't forget, it was his suggestion to meet here, after all.*

No more cars had come into the lot. Had some of these folks taken cabs? The same people sat around the bar chugging away and the two couples at the tables near the opposite wall hadn't moved. He realized he hadn't heard any voices either. Just the music. This was as good of a spot as any to get this story. It was his first time at this bar, but he figured it out quickly. The place was quiet. Calm. A shot-and-a-beer bar after work; a sanctuary for disloyal husbands; a watering hole for depressed salesmen. Why not the site of an exclusive interview with an infamous ballplayer, too? Vinnie returned to his notes and rehearsed.

His glass was about empty.

7:29 PM.

Did Mesnor really forget? Had something happened to him? Was this all bullshit? Vinnie drummed his pencil on his notepad as he looked out at the parking lot. He checked his watch again. Then he got up and ordered another Glenlivet from the bar. Three fingers this time, screw it. He decided he was going to spend big tonight, with or without his interview. If he got it, he'd celebrate. If not, he'd belly up and drown his sorrows with the regulars. The silent bartender poured his drink, then looked up at him with what felt to Vinnie like a knowing smirk. A strand of his slicked black hair fell across his forehead. Vinnie just stared back at the man, unsure what his odd look meant. "Um, thanks," he managed. The bartender glanced over Vinnie's shoulder and walked away without saying a word.

Vinnie turned back toward the booth and stopped mid-step.

Seated on the opposite side of the booth was an elderly man in a gray overcoat. He wore a black derby hat that accentuated large, bright eyes that stared right in his direction. Vinnie glanced around the bar, noting that everyone was still exactly where they had been since he arrived. *The old man obviously snuck in when I was ordering my drink.* Could this be him? The last photos of Pete Mesnor were taken when he was still playing ball. The man in front of him didn't quite look like the elderly version of the once great player, but he supposed it might be him.

The fact the old man knew which booth to go to didn't occur to Vinnie. "Um, hello there, Mister...Mesnor?"

"You bet. Hello Vincent," he said, offering a handshake.

His icy hand nearly crushed Vinnie's own. He didn't expect such a strong grip from a frail man in his late eighties. Then he reminded himself. *Old ballplayer.* Even seated, the man appeared tall. A few whisps of white hair spilled down from his hat behind his ears.

"Didn't see you come in. I thought you may have even forgotten," Vinnie said as he slid into his seat, subtly flexing the pain out of his throbbing hand.

"I was delayed. I apologize." He looked around the bar, a comfortable grin spreading across his weathered face, like he was in his favorite joint. His gray eyes, framed by decades of laugh lines and squinting in sunlit ballparks glared back at Vinnie. "But this old man never forgets anything."

"No worries, sir. Drink?"

Pete regarded Vinnie's scotch and cocked a thick, gray eyebrow upward. Vinnie nodded, getting the hint. "Coming right up," Vinnie said, scooching out of the booth.

He expected to have to get the bartender's attention, so Vinnie was surprised to see him already completing the pour before he even left his seat. He slid it toward the edge of the bar with another nod as if he knew all along what the old man wanted. Vinnie wondered if he might be a regular here. He grabbed the newborn drink and shuffled back to the booth.

"Here you go, Mr. Mesnor, it's on me tonight."

He took a long, slow sip, eyeing Vinnie over the rim of the glass. His expression showed pure contentment. He savored the expensive liquid, the atmosphere, the music and the moment all at once.

"I've read all about you!" Vinnie allowed himself to be starstruck for a moment. He fished out a cigar from his shirt pocket, watching the imposing elderly man for his reaction "Oh! do you mind?"

"Not at all," Pete said. "I used to appreciate a good cigar when I was your age. Takes too long now. Not quite as satisfying."

"I listened to a lot of old sportswriters and fans talk about you too," Vinnie said, flicking his lighter on to start his stogie. Time to celebrate now, he figured. "Ever since I started covering the team, hell, ever since I started learning about the game, every ballplayer has tried to live up to what you did."

Pete squinted at him.

Vinnie knew he gave himself up right then and there.

"On the field," he clarified before taking a sizeable, embarrassing gulp of the scotch, splashing a little down his lower lip.

Pete cocked his head.

Vinnie felt trapped. He'd been talking to the man less than two minutes, and he already screwed up his big chance. He took a deliberately long sip. *Fuck it. The only way out is through, now.* "You were really something else. It's a shame how it all went down."

The instrumental music was louder than before.

"Listen kid," he sighed. "You know how some people just think they know everything?"

Vinnie straightened in his seat as he nodded. Maybe he didn't cock this up after all. He only brought up the situation by accident and here Mesnor was, about to actually tell the story. Vinnie still had lady luck in his corner, after all.

"Well, everybody thinks they're a smart guy about what happened. The truth is, something went down alright, but it wasn't…exactly me." He gave a short, knowing laugh and looked out the window.

Vinnie wanted so badly to ask what he meant, but he decided to allow Mesnor to continue when he was ready.

After a smoky pause, Pete took another slow, appreciative sip – the sip of a connoisseur.

"I remember that last ballgame like it was just this morning. Only a week or so left in the season and most of the boys had wrapped it up by then since we weren't winning the pennant. We could have though. Boy, we had a good club in '11. Just needed a couple of breaks down the stretch. But it didn't happen, so there we were, just playing out the string, you know. Some of the boys were already talking about winning it all next year, you know all that yackin' ballplayers and fans do."

Vinnie smiled and nodded.

"Well, in the middle of the fifth inning the clubhouse kid comes running to the dugout and says some serious boys in suits want to see me. I wasn't due up that inning, so I went down the tunnel to see what the fuss was about. Soon as I got to the clubhouse, they hauled me off right then, still in my uniform, in the middle of the damned game! Someone told the skipper I'd hurt my knee or some other bullshit for the papers."

"They wouldn't even let you change back into your suit?"

The old man shook his head. A mellow jazz tune started playing.

"That's what happens in one of those so called high-profile murders of a famous person, or a politician in that case. I don't know how it is now, but in those days, there was no time for surveillance. Once they found a suspect, they took you as you were. Could've even been in the john for all they cared."

"I guess being in a dusty Pirates uniform would be better than that!" Vinnie said with a chuckle, trying to lighten the talk.

Pete wasn't amused.

He frowned as he swirled his drink. "They had a car parked right outside the players' entrance, one of those new Model T's. Guess they wanted to show me they were all business. Boy, she was a beaut! Almost felt bad about tracking in dirt from my cleats but then I remembered it was their fault for not letting me shower and change, so that was on them. Anyway, off we went to the clink. I kept thinking somebody sure had it out for me. But I knew even if I could prove I was innocent, my career was going to be over. As soon as word hit the papers and the streets, I was all done. There ain't no next inning after that, know what I mean?"

"But you did prove it. They got you mixed up, didn't they? You didn't do a thing. You could've kept –"

56

The old man waved him to silence. Vinnie had sounded like a starstruck fan again, not a reporter trying to reveal the truth. That sparked him to remember something from just a few minutes ago.

"Wait. You said it wasn't 'exactly you' with regard to what went down with the McNeil murder. What does that mean?"

Pete stopped mid-sip and put down his drink. "Nothing that matters now, even if it ever did even then. Some folks can be easily influenced when you put the squeeze on 'em. I'm not one of them. Turn the page, kid."

Crestfallen, Vinnie decided not to push. But there was definitely a detail or two the old ballplayer seemed to hold back. "Well, after you were cleared, you kind of just stepped away completely. Can I ask, what have you been doing for the last 50 years?"

"I wasn't always a ballplayer. I tinkered with trains out east before that. After the problems in Pittsburgh, I took what I had left and melted in among them."

"Them?"

"I knocked around here and there. Played some outlaw ball under another fake name for a while. Took odd jobs," Pete said.

Vinnie hung on to his every word. This is a big part of the story he was hoping to get. "I hung around in New York during the crash. Snuck over to Europe during the War and let me tell you – that was a sight. Played some golf. Visited nowhere towns in nowhere places like Minnesota, Montana and Idaho." He paused for another sip of scotch.

"That sounds like a hell of an adventure!" Vinnie said. "Ever think of writing a biography?"

The old man sat his drink back down. "I was surprised you tracked me down. Good detective work, kid. You must really be intuitive." He leaned over the table toward Vinnie. "Maybe you saw this meeting coming, like I did. The rest, well, now you know the rest."

Vinnie furrowed his brow in surprise. "You saw this coming? And do I really know the rest, other than what you just said? Because it seems you're hiding something." The words came out more aggressively than Vinnie intended. Whiskey bravado. He also unwittingly took the bait with the accusation. Pete stared at him for so long and sternly it was as though he was seeing through him, looking at something else.

The old man leaned back. "You don't know quite as much as I do, Vincent."

"I'm sorry?"

"You oughta be," he said, and smiled at him again.

Vinnie darted his eyes around the table, thinking. "Not sure I follow you, Mr. Mesnor."

Pete sighed, folding his hands on the table. "I'll make you a deal kid. Why don't you ask me what's *really* on your mind, and I'll tell you what you need to know."

Now it was Vinnie's turn to stare. The old man clearly knew something. About Vinnie. Or he's about to make a threat.

"S, sure, Mr. Mesnor."

He flashed a toothy, satisfied grin and nodded. "Go on, kid."

"Y...you h...were in the middle of a great career. Some say you're the best there ever was, even though you should've played a lot longer." Vinnie tried not to sound like a fan again, but the words barfed out faster than his mind could think about what he was going to say. "The story is you're not in the Hall of Fame because of what happened, even though you were found innocent. Why wait all these years to talk? Why not try to clear your name sooner? Running away made it seem like you had something to hide, they say."

"Hiding is either the act of cowards or the work of a genius," Pete said. "I chose to step out of one light into another. It felt better than the dark. Besides, my name can't be cleared. At least, it hasn't been since the beginning of...well, everything. Funny thing about having so many names, you'd think it'd be easier to have a clean image. But soon, very soon, by my measure anyway, it might be."

Vinnie pursed his lips, his head cocked. He had no idea where Mesnor was going with this cryptic talk. It was almost as if he'd been talking to himself.

"You see kid, we're all headed to an end," he continued. "Some are...drearier than others. They say the ends justify the means but once upon a time I didn't buy into that. Still not sure that I really do. Everything according to His plan and all that jazz. But plans can change. Maybe people can too."

Vinnie was too busy scribbling in his notebook to decipher this nonsense. He'd figure it out later. Busy with his own note taking, he didn't notice that Pete had scribbled something of his own on a cocktail napkin and hid its folded content in his large hand. Three drinks didn't calm Vinnie's nerves, but they sure had loosened his tongue. "I don't believe you did what they said," he blurted out. "I think it was all just a bunch of bullshit to be honest. Why would anyone throw everything away, while still in his prime, no less? Any man does that he'd have to be crazy or...possessed or something."

The old man looked at Vinnie with a new gleam in his gold eyes.

"What is it, Mr. Mesnor? You ok?"

Pete took another sip, set his glass down and smiled to himself. "You know, you're smarter than you lead on, kid. Though I guess you'd have to be to hide what you hid. Right, Vincent Penino?"

A chill bolted up Vinnie's spine and sent him into a shiver. It was both what he said and how he said it.

"W…what do you mean?"

"I told you, kid. I'll tell you what you need to know. And right now, my young friend, you need to know that while you don't believe what they said *I* did, I know what *you really* did."

Flustered, Vinnie swirled his glass and looked around the room, checking for ears as much as eyes. "I'm just a reporter," he said, lowering his voice to a whisper. "I didn't do anything. Come on now, Mr. Mesnor, let's get back to baseball. I read all about the doubleheader in Philly when you hit four grand slams, two in each – "

"Don't change the subject Vincent. Time is almost up. For me, them, and you."

"Why do you keep calling me Vincent?" He forced a chuckle. "Nobody calls me that, except – "

"Your lovely parents, right? But of course."

"Right," Vinnie let out a whiskey-soaked sigh. "Good guess."

"And Loretta Danforth did, too."

Vinnie felt his insides turn to mush. He sat perfectly still, mouth agape, waiting for Pete to say something more. His mind flashed back to that night all those years ago, unable to think of an excuse that would fit in the present. His wondered if his silence betrayed his guilt. Vinnie opened his mouth, but Pete raised a hand before he could speak.

"Yeah, I know all about that," Pete said. We get all the news downstairs. Tsk, tsk, tsk. Poor Loretta. Back in '47 was it? Yeah, Minnesota. That's it. A no-name postulant in one of those no-name towns I loved to visit. Nice church, though. Gone way too soon. Such a shame. They said it was an accident, of course. But we know better, don't we, Vincent?"

The song on the jukebox changed again. Something sad and bluesy.

Vinnie quenched his now parched throat with the rest of his scotch in one long, slow gulp.
"I have no idea what you're – "

Pete smacked a silencing slap on the tabletop. "Tell you what, Chum. You chew on that for a minute while I hit the john. I'll get us another round on the way back and then maybe we can talk this out." The thin, elderly man hopped up with a surprising grace. "Be right back." Vinnie stared at him in disbelief as Pete walked with a curious fluidity, almost gliding toward the bathroom door.

Vinnie felt bolted to his seat. Unable to move. Barely able to breathe. His body flushed hot. How could this man – a man he's never met – a famous baseball player, possibly know about what happened in Swan River all those years ago?

An urge to leave shot through Vinnie like electric shock. He stirred from his seat. He knew he had to get out of there *now*, that very moment. Something tugged at him, whether it was the guilt over the incident, or fear, he didn't care. He snatched up his hat and stood to make a dash for it when he noticed Pete's cocktail napkin on the table, it practically jumped out at him.

SHE HAD A DAUGHTER.
SEE YOU DOWNSTAIRS

Vinnie grabbed at his chest; his breath reduced to ragged gasps. Beads of sweat popped on his forehead and ran down the back of his neck. He could already feel his shirt getting damp. It was then that he got his first clear look at the faces in the bar. They finally acknowledged him. But something looked wrong. Their eyes were vivid, almost glowing with unnatural brightness against the subtle light in the establishment. The room spun. Vinnie staggered, catching himself on the edge of booth. Something outside the window caught his attention. He saw Pete, who was not in the bathroom but out in the parking lot, staring right back in at him. He doffed his hat toward Vinnie, sending a long mane of silver-gray hair cascading down over his shoulders.

~ * ~

TAVERN EXPLOSION UPDATE
Erie, Pennsylvania, November 14, 1960 – Area officials combed through the charred remains of Bev's Tavern on Morningstar Road in southern Erie after an explosion completely destroyed the establishment last Thursday evening. No human remains have been discovered and it is unclear as to how many patrons were inside at the time of the incident. Only one vehicle was found in the parking lot, a blue 1955 Buick Century. Investigators are in the process of determining whom it belongs to.

Given the degree of destruction, the initial investigation ascertains it was an explosion of extreme magnitude and heat. Residents as far Fairview claim to have heard the boom just before 8pm. Debris samples from the site have been taken to Omicron Laboratory in upstate New York for analysis to try and determine the cause of the explosion.
This story will be updated.

~ * ~

Signals

Ted swatted the ball with the power of a tour pro. His shots were unusually strong and accurate. A layup with the 8-iron would've been the conventional approach, but he felt aggressive with a 2-stroke lead. Shielding his eyes from the hazy late morning sunlight, he watched the smooth flight of the ball arc downward and *plap* safely onto the 10th green. "FORE!" he yelled.

Startled by the near miss, the three people finishing their putts on the 10th turned towards him, arms stretched wide. "Hey man, what the fuck?" one shouted.

"Jesus, Ted! Are you *trying* to hit those guys?" Jim asked.

"Well, shit the bed! They need to putt faster, or—"

Jim raised an arm. "Or you need to swing softer."

He'd hit his stride at the 5th hole. By the 10th he was on cruise control. For Ted Crabtree, aka "Crabby", the nickname Jim gave him in their Army years, lazy days on the course were his favorite pastime. He played just for fun, but to his opponents, his taunting verbiage and beer muscles had a tendency to make the outings feel more competitive than they needed to be.

He wore his lucky brown plaid pants, and, fueled by a couple breakfast Schlitzes, Ted was beaming. By the time they sunk their last putts of the day, he didn't even try to hide his cocky grin. "As usual, losers buy the first *two* rounds at the 19th hole!"

Jim shook his head as he removed his trusty golf glove. "Two damned strokes. That's all it took, otherwise I had your arrogant ass! It was the sand trap on 11 that did it."

"Yeah, and the pond on nine. And I lost count how many times you hooked or sliced. Either way, I win, again."

Jim stared out at the course. "And I never slice."

The two buddies shared a chuckle as they set their clubs against the wall near the polished wooden door and strolled into the clubhouse, eager to knock back a few after a tightly contested round on the links. Several other golfers and their guests sat at the long mahogany bar, with another pair munching on overpriced sandwiches and soggy tater tots at a nearby table.

"Hiya, Claire!" Jim always greeted the bartender warmly. He had known Claire even longer than Ted, as their sisters grew up as good friends.

She grinned at him. "Hey Jimbo, how'd it go out there?" Her sarcastic tone indicated she knew the answer.

"Ha!" Ted interjected, giving his friend a nudge. "Jimmy Singer loses again."

"Got him, eh, Crabby?" Claire asked, as she set her two regulars' beers on the bar. Ted flashed a thumbs up.

"Heard the new Beatles album?" Jim asked.

"Bought two copies last week! Best one yet! Oh, that Paul," she said dreamily. The guys rolled their eyes in unison. "Oh, Ted that reminds me," she said, snapping out of her reverie. "This arrived for you this morning. I was going to give it to you earlier, but you guys had already bolted to the tee." She grabbed a blue-and-gold striped envelope from beside the register and slid it across the bar top toward him.

Ted furrowed his brow as he picked up the comical-looking parcel. "What's this?"

"Jerry said it was in the mailbox when he got in this morning." Claire shrugged. "Must've been delivered overnight."

Ted wondered what it could be. Other than Jim, only Gayle knew he was golfing today. He'd never received any packages there before. He took a long swig of his cold lager, holding the hoppy liquid for a moment as he stared at the envelope. He gulped back his sip as he glanced around the clubhouse to see if anyone was watching him. Then someone at a side table caught his eye. Ted watched with equal parts amusement and disgust as a rotund man in a peach-colored button-down ignored the greasy tater tot that rolled off his plate to the fairway-green carpet. He paid no attention to the sizable splotch of cheese on his noisy shirt either.

He tore the envelope open and pulled out a small, folded piece of yellowing paper. A short message was written in bold, felt marker:

WATCH - SIGNALS
3

He smirked at Jim, thinking he had pulled some prank.

"What is it?" Jim asked, nodding toward the letter.

"I don't know. *You* wouldn't either I assume?" Ted asked with an accusatory look.

Jim just tilted his head toward him, as if to say Ted should know better.

Claire moaned angrily from behind the bar. "Ah, shit!" Ted and Jim looked up to see a whole bottle of ketchup lying the wrong way, its contents pooled on the countertop.

"Oh, good job, Claire!" Jim teased, then looked in askance again at Ted.

"No idea," Ted said. "Weird. Oh well, probably some mistake." He folded the note back in the envelope and used it as a coaster. "Claire, did Jerry say anything else about the delivery? Was he expecting any special parcel besides the regular mail?"

Claire called over her shoulder as she wiped up the saucy mess on the counter. "Not that I know of." She tossed the soiled paper towels in the trash can with a *plop* and walked back over to Ted. "It is a little strange that someone would deliver that in the middle of the night though, we usually don't get the mail or any other deliveries until at least noon."

"Is Jerry still around?"

"No, he left this morning to head up to Harland Falls. Won't be back until Sunday."

Ted nodded. Something obviously didn't add up, but there wasn't much he could do about it. Has to be some kind of a joke. An early birthday gag, he guessed. Jim pulled out his scorecard and shook his head, still upset over the handful of holes that cost him the game. Ted, noticing, chuckled. He downed the rest of his winning beer in one gulp and signaled Claire to grab another round.

~ * ~

The Monday workday came and went without surprise, though despite his best efforts to avoid it, Ted kept thinking about the strange letter he received at the golf course. That's the problem with managing security at the bank, Ted realized. Too much time to think, but he couldn't complain. His Army pension allowed him to get out of his supervisor's role at the refinery, and he enjoyed the flexibility and the quiet of the security job. It kept him active and afforded him plenty of time to golf. He and Gayle just celebrated their twentieth anniversary. They had built the life they dreamed of.

By Thursday, Ted had forgotten all about the weird letter and was excited for the weekend. He pulled his prized Plymouth into the driveway just after 5 o'clock. When he got out of the car he noticed, with mild annoyance, Gayle visiting the neighbors across the street, a lovely young married couple. She'd been spending more time with them the past few weeks. More time with all the neighbors, Ted realized. It didn't seem like she was organizing another block party either, unless it was the best kept secret in the neighborhood this time. He watched them from the rearview mirror. The three of them were laughing about something, which made the suspicion in his gut start to rise. He couldn't convince himself he had nothing to worry about; he was trained to be ever vigilant during the war. He hopped out of his dark blue machine and walked toward the street, giving an emotionless wave to the chatting trio.

"Hi, hon!" Gayle shouted, out of breath from her giggling. "Can you grab the mail? I'll be there in a minute."

Ted nodded absently, feeling left out. For a fleeting instant he thought of walking over to join the conversation, but if he already felt like an outsider to their little club from a distance; it might be worse up close. He pulled the contents from the mailbox, flipping through the batch of letters on his way into the house. The fourth one in the pile made him stop in his tracks.

An envelope with blue and gold stripes.

He glanced back at Gayle, still talking with the neighbors on the sidewalk. Down the block, a group of children were engaged in a game of hopscotch. Satisfied nobody was watching him, he opened the circus tent-looking envelope. A familiar piece of paper with equally familiar handwriting rested within. The message made even less sense than the first one.

PUPPETS AND STRINGS AND NASTY THINGS
ITS ALL A GAME

3 CHIMES - OUT OF TIME

Okay, what's this about? Ted's prior bemused curiosity now gave way to sheer annoyance. *What game? What chimes?* His heart pounded with fresh frustration. He gritted his teeth and stared at his wife and neighbors, looking for any hint they were in on this gag. They all seemed oblivious to his presence. He pocketed the note and dropped the colorful envelope in the trash can next to the garage.

"Dinner is in the oven, hon!" Gayle called out, joining Ted as he was walking into their cozy two-story. She kissed him. "Good day?" she asked.

"Fine. How are you dear? What's happening across the street?"

"Oh nothing, just chit chat. I was watering the flowers out front when they walked by. The roast is just about ready!" Ted watched his wife waltz off to the kitchen. A dark suspicion rose like bile. The garden hose was in its usual spot on the side of the garage, and the flower bed looked dry as a bone.

Ted was uncommunicative during dinner. Usually, Gayle could barely get a word in, but Ted hardly spoke. His mind kept running in circles thinking of who had been sending the strange letters and why. Was it someone at work or the country club? Or did he not give Jim enough credit as a prankster? And why did Gayle just lie to him?

He wished he could care less, but he couldn't help himself. He rolled a pile of green beans back and forth on his plate as his analytical senses once again kicked into gear. All those years working in U.S. Army Intelligence had taught him to question everything. To be intentionally suspicious. He'd wanted infantry when he joined – two years and done. Nice and quick. But some random question on some aptitude test somewhere landed him in the intelligence office, analyzing classified-everything from radio communications and military movements to the purely bizarre – like that Schweinfurt mission in '43.

That's where it all started, Ted realized. He set his fork down and stared at his plate. Past his plate. Through the table, the floor, and into 23 years in the past.

It was a hell of a first case for a green officer. Major Briggs, someone Ted hadn't seen before – or since – that day, assigned it to him. His orders were to figure out how a nearly destroyed bomber with three engines inoperable and both pilots dead seemingly landed itself. At first it wasn't really shocking. Those B-17's were famous for being able to take a real beating and keep flying. Except some of the survivors of this particular plane kept rattling in hysterics about some other man who was at the controls after everyone with flying experience onboard was killed. Eventually it was chalked up to hallucinations from blood loss at altitude and battle fatigue. Nobody in the office ever came to any solid conclusion about that case. The surviving crew disappeared shortly after that mission. World War II officially ended a couple years later. But Ted always felt something was off about the survivors' accounts. He didn't believe in the dumb luck of it, nor that the crew hallucinating was as cut and dried as the Eighth Air Force wanted it to be. Something terrified them up there, beyond the mission itself.

Ever since, Ted watched *everything* with even more curious eyes, harboring a secret belief that someone, somewhere was always orchestrating things.

"Ted! What's wrong?" Gayle snapped.

Ted blinked. "Hmm. Oh, nothing. Was just remembering something from work." He felt a twinge of silliness. Perhaps he was overthinking this. Or maybe there really *was* something wrong out there.

"Well, you spaced out. I have a cake ready for dessert," Gayle said as she grabbed up their dishes and spun toward the sink. Ted checked his watch, then drummed a few fingers across the table. He refolded his napkin across his lap. He couldn't sit on this any longer.

"Hon, have you noticed any strange mail lately? Or are any of your friends pulling some kind of prank? Maybe someone spreading odd messages around town?"

Gayle placed a hand on his forehead. "Geez, dear, are you okay?"

"I'm serious."

"I can see that. It's really starting to worry me." There wasn't a trace of concern in her voice.

Ted cocked an eyebrow. He gave her a chance to be straight with him, but the dismissal remained in her voice. Gayle was a hugely caring woman. If Ted so much as sneezed, she'd immediately start making chicken soup. Why the nonchalance now?

"You've seen or heard nothing at all?"

"Afraid not. I think you've been spending too much time at the 'fromper' lately. What are you getting at?"

And there it is. He slammed a fist against his knee. Ted despised that little nickname she gave his favorite restaurant, a rustic, all-you-can-eat joint serving eastern European faire. Yes, Carpathian Fromphaus was a silly name. But he loved the food and the unique beers they had on tap. It was a good hangout after work. Every time Gayle referred to it as the "fromper" Ted got more incensed.

Gayle set two slices of her famous German chocolate cake down on the table and poured each of them a cup of steaming-hot decaf. The warm, inviting aroma made him forget his anger.

"Nothing, I guess. Never mind, hon. Just a joke, probably from the guys at work."

Ted took a bite of the cake. It was devilishly good.

~*~

Friday the 14ᵗʰ

Ted left the bank right at 5 o'clock to go meet Jim for a few beers. He thought happy hour was just what he needed to clear his mind as he raced to his favorite joint. Carpathian Fromphaus was already buzzing with the after-work and early dinner crowd when he arrived. Jim waived him over to a table near the bar, where he had an order of cheesy broccoli-and-black-bean dip appetizers at the ready. The two fellas devoured them in record time, barely speaking a word to each other. It always felt like time moved a little differently on Friday evenings. Happy hour at Carpathian Fromphaus was always a relaxing scene and Ted fell into his comfort zone.

The two friends leaned back in their chairs as a waitress set down another round of hard-to-pronounce German ales in old style wooden tankards. All of a sudden, a boisterous, awkwardly comical trumpet number blasted in the dining area – the restaurant's proprietary gag heralding the arrival of a certain main course. Ted never knew which menu item triggered the horn blast, but he smiled anyway. He could smell his hearty grub from across the room, some kind of strange combination of hickory smoked, lemon-tinged beef sauce served over chicken with poppyseeds. The server was setting their plates down when Ted considered asking Jim if he'd been noticing anything funny around town lately, or at the course. But the inviting aromas of his dish made him lose his train of thought.

"How's Gayle? Haven't seen her in a bit," Jim asked.

"She's good, I guess. Keeping busy at the library. She has a new hobby of collecting things for some reason. Little trinkets and shit, like statuary. She really loves this green crystal thing she got on our vacation last year. I don't know what it is. It sat in the closet for a long time, but lately she seems obsessed with it. Claims it blesses the house and wards off evil spirits and all that nonsense. Who knows? She's been acting pretty odd lately now that I think of it."

"Crystals huh? Is she getting all cosmic on you?"

"Getting all-something that's for sure," Ted said. "But other than that, she's good."

They scarfed their food as though they were stoned. Then, between oversized bites of his braised oxtails and spiced cabbage, Jim dropped his fork. It bounced off his plate with a sharp *ting*.

Ted looked up. Jim stared mischievously at his friend.

"What is it?" Ted asked.

Jim darted his eyes around the room suspiciously, as if he was about to reveal a secret. He then leaned slowly to one side, gave a quick grunt and released what sounded like a week's worth of gas. The groaning noise was sharp. Desert dry. Amplified by the wooden chair. Ted sat across the table in a stupor. Despite the ambient noise, there was no way most, if not all, patrons in the vintage eatery didn't hear Jim's roisterous intestinal relief. But there were no comments, no laughter. Either people miraculously didn't hear or just didn't care. A muffled applause came from a far corner. Jim covered his mouth and was visibly shaking. His face was beet red.

"You have no shame," Ted said.

Jim caught his breath, shrugging off his laughing riot. "We're at the Fromphaus, aren't we?"

A waitress dropped a pack of Simethicone tablets on the table in front of Jim as she walked by. He'd apparently had an audience after all.

It was just after eight o'clock when Ted arrived back home. Gayle sat at the kitchen table, pouring over the evening edition. Two perfectly portioned plates of her homemade meatloaf with mashed potatoes and peas sat cold on the table.

She didn't look up at Ted when he walked in.

"Long day at work huh?" Her voice was flat.

"Sorry dear, Jim and I stopped for a beer and then got to talking and had a few more beers and you know how it goes. I just lost track of time."

He kissed her on the cheek. "This looks delicious as always!"

"Don't start with that, Ted," she snapped. "I know where you and Jim were. That damned European place again, weren't you?"

Ted sighed, prepared for the onslaught. He walked to the refrigerator and grabbed a can of beer.

She side-eyed him. "Yeah, that's it alright. I smelled the stinky cabbage the second you walked in. It's stuck to your clothes like horseflies on a Texas turd!" Ted bit his cheek. "I don't know what you see in that place, anyway. Carpathian Fromphaus can take a hike. Might as well call it 'Fart house' or 'Shithouse'! What the hell is 'Fromphaus' anyway? Sounds like another name for a bathroom."

Ted, still staring at the refrigerator door, hid his smile from Gayle. He knew better than to act amused when she was ranting like this. She could be a pistol, and he loved that about her.

"And that's fitting anyway with how much time people spend there after eating at that dump! Nothing but a bunch of gas-ridden, bloviating buffoons – "

"Okay, honey!" Ted shot back. "I'm sorry, okay?" He stifled a laugh. "Yes, I like the food. Yes, Jim and I had a few too many and stayed out late. And yes, I'm sorry for all of it. Look. It's Friday, dear. You've been acting pretty odd lately if I may say so. Kind of distant. And now you seem to have a problem with the places I go. Is the golf course next on your shitlist? The bank? The garage?" Ted waited for a reply. When Gayle remained silent, he moved toward the front porch and his awaiting rocking chair, then turned back to his wife. "It's going to be lovely out the next few days. Can't we just relax and enjoy the weekend?"

Gayle stood and walked right past Ted to the stairs. "Enjoy it while *you* can," she called over her shoulder as she headed upstairs. Ted took a long swing of beer as he heard his bedroom door slam shut upstairs.

~*~

The third floor of the Oakville Public Library, home to history, medical and rare book collections, was Gayle's favorite spot at work. It always felt bigger on this level somehow. More spacious despite the clutter. Rows and rows of shelves packed with faded, heavy tomes took up most of the level. Gayle always marveled at the vast number of ancient books. It bordered on the absurd. It was the type of collection one would find in big city libraries, not an old hotel-turned-library in forgotten towns.

Gayle always loved the quiet and she felt proud to work with literal treasure. It was nearing the 7PM closing time. Summer hours. Tuesdays were usually slow anyway, and even more now with school out, making it the perfect time for sizeable projects. Gayle looked forward to reorganizing this entire floor and putting up new displays in time for school to start up again in September.

She was busy shifting volumes of Eastern European history on the shelf. The normally quiet tap of setting books, even the heavy ones, on the shelf sounded far louder than usual. She'd never fully appreciated how quiet it could be up here when she was alone. She slid another volume into place and turned to grab another book when she heard another sound.

A voice.

"Hello? Is someone there?" she asked.

The silence returned. Gayle waited. She slowly reached down to her cart and picked up another heavy, tan-covered volume. She was sure she was alone. Nobody else had been up there all day except for Susan, the young part-time desk clerk.

The voice spoke again. A man's. Deep. Smooth and quiet. "You know where I am."

"Oh, my God."

"He isn't here. Now listen."

The voice sounded like it came from directly above her. Though she was alone, she stared up in rapt attention. "I…I can't." Captivated by the voice, she didn't notice Susan had come upstairs with a new stack of books. She peeked around the corner at Gayle, watching with concern as she appeared to be talking to herself. "I can't do this," Gayle said.

He spoke slowly and softly, a perfect library voice. "You know what needs to be done. It's who you want to be, of course. Otherwise, I'd be tending to business elsewhere. There is no redemption without conviction, my dear. Shhh."

She stood teary-eyed and trembling. Susan rushed toward her, tying her long blonde hair into a messy ponytail, something she did when she felt nervous. "Gayle! Are you okay?"

Gayle tried to blink away from her shock, straightening her blouse. "Oh! Yes, yes, I'm fine dear. Just a little moment, there. I thought I'd forgotten something downstairs."

"Oh, well it looks like everything for the church history display is here." Susan let go of her ponytail, crossing her arms instead. "Be straight with me, Mrs. Crabtree. What happened?"

"Nothing!" Gayle surprised herself at her abruptness. She took a deep breath. "Nothing, hon, really. I'm fine. I should really have you handle this display; you're the expert on old churches and religious objects, after all," she said with a smile.

Susan nodded. "We all have our passions. Maybe my mission is important reliquary," she said with an unconvincing shrug.

"Well, your historical, magic objects can wait until tomorrow. Why don't you go get ready to close up? I'll be right down." Susan nodded, dismissing any concern as she left her stack near the shelf and headed back downstairs.

With a sigh, Gayle leaned against the overfilled shelf.

The voice returned.

"Good. Think she bought your little charade? *That* one is dangerous."

Gayle forced a laugh. "She's a sweet girl who just started here, I wouldn't worry—"

"I don't. But maybe you should."

As the voice spoke, a chair bumped out from the table near where she stood, moved by an unseen hand. Gayle looked about the space, relenting to the hint as she slowly sat down.

"Relax, pet. You'll be fine as long as you do as I say," the voice said. "Remember, I'm watching."

"Why me?" Gayle asked.

No answer came, which was somehow worse. She asked the question again. And again.

Silence.

But maybe you should.

Remember, I'm watching.

Gayle rose, scooped up the book she'd meant to shelve and inched out of the stacks, glancing in each direction, confirming she was still alone. Suddenly, the realization of her question arrived, as a wave of adrenaline shot through her. In a confused panic, Gayle dropped the book and ran down the back stairwell, leaving her half-filled cart among the shelves.

Downstairs, Susan was busy closing the register and stacking the evening's paperwork on the desk. Next to the organized pile sat a volume she'd been studying, *A Treatise on Theological Symbolism.* She tucked it in her bag just as Gayle burst through the staff door at the bottom of the stairs and into the lobby, walk-jogging toward the foyer. Susan watched in surprise as she flung the front doors open and bolted into the night.

On the drive home, Gayle's trembling hands and a foot that felt heavy against the pedals made it difficult to drive – and think – straight. She'd hoped he was gone for good, but she knew now that she couldn't elude him.

Her mind raced back to her trip with Ted last year to Costa Rica. It was their last night of vacation, an early celebration for their twentieth anniversary. With some money left to spend, Gayle found a charming antique store near the resort they stayed at – a perfect place to grab some unique gifts for family and friends, she thought. She bought postcards, local coffee beans, and a few pieces of handmade jewelry. After paying for the items, the nice Spanish-speaking woman who seemed to own the store surprised Gayle when she set a heavy green crystal in her bag. She refused payment for it. Gayle didn't even want it but couldn't deny its beauty. "Just take it. A gift," the lady had said, eyes wide and smiling. It seemed to be the only English she knew.

Two weeks later, he approached her at the library's fundraiser gala. He was startling, not just in the way he appeared but also in his look – tall, wearing a tailored suit, long silver-blonde hair pulled back tight, frighteningly handsome, strong. He spoke calmly but cryptically and made little sense except for one thing that Gayle had not forgotten. She played the words over and over in her head, like a memorable lyric to a beloved song. It wasn't his nursery rhyme delivery that scared her, but rather that she knew, instinctively, what the words meant.

A quiet end for those who know
But after the three, all will go

It was just past a quarter after seven when Gayle entered the house. She closed the door and leaned back against it with a *thud*. She took a deep breath. The house smelled like salt and garlic, with a slightly burned accent. And something starchy. Ted's pork chops. Immediately she felt lighter.

"Hon? That you? I have dinner ready!" Ted called out.

She walked into the warm kitchen where Ted was finishing setting two plates featuring his self-proclaimed famous pork chops topped with apple-onion chutney and a plump side of garlic mashed potatoes. She had to admit, Ted had some cooking talent. Maybe he picked up a thing or two at the Craphouse or whatever it was.

"You're a peach, dear. It looks wonderful!"

Gayle eyed Ted as he rinsed his prep dishes and utensils in the sink. She couldn't decide if the surprise dinner was an apology for spending time away from her lately, or if he was just doing a nice thing since she was working late. Either way, it didn't matter. This was a good thing.

All of a sudden, Gayle snapped her eyes shut. She reached out her hand and grabbed the back of a chair to steady herself. She swayed in a half circle, as though massively drunk.

"You okay, hon?" Ted bolted to her, holding her shoulders steady.

"Yes! Fine! I just remembered –" She sighed, blinking rapidly. "It's nothing. Maybe just a little hungrier than I thought," she said as she looked around the table, calculating. "I'm fine now. Oh! We need salads. I'll tell you what, you go relax and have a drink, and I'll make those since you did all the rest. Homemade dressing!" Ted grinned wide, both with excitement and relief. He grabbed a fresh peach from the fruit bowl on the counter and held it out pleadingly. "Yes," she laughed. "Your favorite."

Ted kissed Gayle on the cheek and went out to the living room. Gayle began peeling and pitting the fruit to make Ted's favorite peach vinaigrette. After she gathered the ingredients, she peeked into the living room where Ted was sipping a glass of scotch and reading the evening paper. "Just a few minutes, dear!" she called, partly in truth but mostly so he wouldn't come back to the kitchen. Gayle loved cooking and baking for others, but she enjoyed the process more if she was alone. It was her meditation. She finished mixing the dressing and set the table just as Ted reappeared in the kitchen with his empty glass.

They sat down and enjoyed the perfect dinner. The evening passed pleasurably for both of them, melting away some of the tensions from the past week.

~*~

Ted woke up Wednesday morning and made his way to work feeling a bit off. Not really sick, just a little congested. By lunchtime he had broken out in a light sweat. He figured he was just catching a cold and concentrated on his duties.

By Friday, Ted could barely move without pain. His eyes were blurry. He vomited twice before lunch. His head throbbed and his back ached. He hated to miss happy hour, but he felt in no condition to go anywhere after work. He should've called in sick, but Fridays were usually busy at the bank, especially during lunchtime. He believed he could stick it out. Army tough to the end. Early in the afternoon, after the midday throng thinned out, a tall man in a fine tailored suit entered the bank. He approached Ted, who leaned against the corner checking counter, exhausted. He stood several feet away, staring in Ted's direction with determined eyes. Ted looked away, unsure if this man was regarding him or the clock on the wall behind him. Finally, Ted locked eyes with the stranger. He opened his mouth to speak but was cut off.

"Fruit shouldn't be so bitter this time of year, wouldn't you say, Sergeant Crabtree?" he said.

"Wh – what? I'm not a sergeant anymore, Mr.?"

"Who I am is a long story, and I'm afraid we have nowhere near the time. What I want, or rather, what is about to happen to you for what you saw is very important. You see, you were close back there, Teddy boy. Oh, so close. If only you didn't shrug off your belief."

Ted straightened up the best he could. His voice was gravelly. "What are you talking about? How do you know my name?"

"I was there, you might say. You saw it back in '43, didn't you? All that confused testimony had a commonality, didn't it? And smart little *Teddy Bear* – that childhood nickname you always hated – weaved it all together. You should trust your gut like that more often if it wasn't melting inside you right now. See, I want to make it seem as though nobody remembers what happened on that day."

Ted stared in disbelief at the excited visitor who clasped his hands together and grinned back at him. "It was an ugly one, wasn't it? All that destruction and pain and burning," he said. "We really cashed in downstairs. Frightfully entertaining. Lucky for you." He chuckled. "Pardon the pun there. We, well. We won't meet again. I just wanted to do you the honor of showing you who'd been nudging you along all these years. Enjoy, Teddy Bear." The man tipped his hat toward Ted and turned to leave.

"Hold it!" Ted shouted, but it came out like a hoarse whisper. He stepped toward him on wobbly legs and attempted to brandish his nightstick. It slipped through a sweaty palm and *clacked* against the tile floor, drawing startled looks from those in the bank. Sensing eyes on him and not wanting to cause a scene, Ted whispered. He retrieved his nightstick and held it at his side. "Who the fuck are you? What do you want with me?"

"Not a thing, my friend," the man said, palms raised in defense. "Not anymore, at least. You're just the example. But Gayle, now she's a firecracker, isn't she?"

He rocked on his heels, whistling softly. When Ted didn't respond, he shook his head slowly. "Gullible as a fucking schoolchild though. Not to mention flaunting property that doesn't belong to her…and that she can't comprehend. Tell me, Ted. Do you believe, as she does, that a little crystal bauble can really *ward off* the bad things out there?"

Ted burped back a thick wave of bile – or worse. The bathroom door was only steps away, just behind the man. But he knew he needed a hospital. Fast. He struggled to form a response. Then he looked right at the man. "Evil comes and goes as it pleases, I think."

The man laughed heartily, clapping his hands and drawing more curious looks from bankers and employees. "Oh Ted, you really are the smart one, despite what your lovely wife says. Don't you see that's why I've been trying to *warn* you? You figured things out once before, and I thought you would again with my help. You were so good at deciphering strange messages once."

"You sent those letters?" Ted grimaced, his sweat dotting the floor beneath him.

Bob, the stuffy, slick-haired bank manager noticed the conversation – and Ted's distressing appearance.

"Ted," he called out. Everything okay? You look – "

"All good here, Bob!" Ted shot back.

The stranger looked pleased. "Well, aren't you just as clever as your golf pants? You finally figured it out. But I was wrong this time."

The man adjusted the brim on his dress hat, giggling as he swept a lock of silver-blonde hair behind his ear. "Well, before I go, here's one for you, Teddy. Some little charms really *do* work. Especially the ones that call me instead of shooing me off. Like that precious table decoration your wife has. Why do you think the seller was so eager to be rid of it?" He waved a hand, as if dismissing his own remark. "No matter. Through you, she'll learn of her mistake the hard way. Don't worry, though. I'll take good care of her."

The man turned and walked swiftly out of the bank. Ted tried to call after him, but he stumbled and doubled over, grimacing. He limped back to clutch the counter, trailing sweat like breadcrumbs. The pain in his body nearly equaled his anger and feeling of being betrayed by the person he loved most in the world.

Ted gathered himself as best he could. He smoothed out his sweat-soaked shirt and lurched over to the front desk. He told Bob, the stuffy, slick-haired bank manager, that he had to leave. He nodded at Ted's wet, pale face and told him he hoped he felt better.

~*~

Gayle sat on the new porch swing Ted had just hung up that spring, doing a crossword puzzle from the morning paper. The silky smooth voice she knew so well pierced her quiet mind.

"Now, let me tell you the rest of the plan."

The faint wails of emergency sirens echoed somewhere across town. Gayle didn't even realize she was smiling.

~*~

Caedis

Too few have heeded the warnings – even those we've placed in their own hearts.

Fewer still now believe.

It is time to bring the charge to judgement according to His law.

Trust in Him to have mercy, lest the arrival of the end.

– J

The Gift That Keeps on Taking

Alana paced around her rather generic-looking suburban kitchen, dusting and straightening. She must've scrubbed the same section of Formica countertop for the third time. It's off-white color was both basic and ugly, the kind that could drive someone crazy wrestling with whether it was stained, faded, or if someone really invented the godforsaken color on purpose. She frowned at a new chip on the surface, hoping it won't turn into a full-fledged crack. That's when she wondered if she were becoming *actually* crazy. But given how the last seven months had gone, the stress was bound to catch up sooner or later.

She left the kitchen, but not before resetting the microwave and the oven clocks to precisely the same time. Then she checked every other clock in the house, desperate to focus her energy anywhere than her own head. Before leaving her bedroom, she glanced out the window. That was it. The mild, sunny day was too rare for November to waste cooped up inside any longer, especially on a day off from work.

She popped in her earbuds, strolled out her front door and turned up the sidewalk. The heat from the summer had long gone away, but on this day, so had the cold bite of autumn. The sun warmed but didn't burn and the breeze felt cool on her skin without annoyance. She waived at her elderly next-door neighbor who sat on her porch, too engrossed in a hardcover to see Alana walk past. It was a good day for clearing one's mind, and Alana sure had a lot of clutter up there. Her newest divorce had been less rocky than the first one, all things considered. But it was still a major life change that needed sorting out. Fortunately, the beautiful reds, oranges, and yellows of the season brought a smile to her face.

Alana Reyes didn't experience this drastic of a change in nature growing up in Costa Rica. It was something she grew to love about the different seasons ever since her father's job forced her family to relocate to the area when she was fourteen. She didn't even mind the cold, harsh winters. It was so different than the weather near Nosara which only seemed to have two seasons – furnace or monsoon. Energized by the music, the weather, and a budding sense of enthusiasm, Alana smiled as she picked up her pace and headed south down her own sloping Whitford Avenue. She mimed the lyrics to the old Ray Charles number that was playing in her ears, not even realizing she had done so. At the corner, she playfully kicked a small leaf pile before turning up Eaglewood, lined with its massive oak trees. The earthen, stale-sweet scent of the autumn air seemed to grow even stronger as she walked across to Bell, and then Westshire, once the avenue of the wealthy in the town's early days. Upon each side of the pockmarked street stood many mansions of old: Queen Anne's, Victorians, Tudors, Traditionals – all in varying stages of upkeep but still resplendent with a haunting, ages-old beauty. Alana thought the Victorian's were particularly stunning with their gingerbread-lined eaves and three-story rounded turrets. The well-to-do owners of some of the more restored homes enclosed their leaf-strewn lawns in ornate, wrought iron fences. Just because they could.

The sun began to set just after 4 o'clock, filtering golden shivelight through the trees and throwing playful shadows along the ground. Although she'd walked these streets countless times, she always loved looking at the detailed architecture from a bygone era that many of the houses featured. The late afternoon light gave it all a picturesque quality that made her feel a joyful connection to the neighborhood, like remembering a good dream. While looping back down Westshire, she raised her arm to shield her eyes against the setting sun and caught the fading tan line on her wrist. A reminder of her missing watch – a gift from coworkers at the hospital with her name scripted across its pewter face – dulled some of the day's enjoyment. Despite searching high and low, she just couldn't find where she had left it. When she completed her neighborhood lap, she went right to the house next door to see Mrs. Crabtree. She was still sitting on the old wooden bench swing on her front porch when she glanced up from her book.

"Hello Alana, my dear!"

"Hi, Gayle, how are you today?"

"Oh, just fine. No problems, and if there were...bah, I'd just sweep 'em under the rug!" she exclaimed with a wave of her hand, her customary quip.

She patted a spot on the swing next to her. "Come on up here, grab a seat. Enjoy this beautiful day!"

Alana obliged. For the day was beautiful and Mrs. Gayle Crabtree was a lovely woman. She was a widow somewhere in her early nineties, but full of robust energy and vigor. Snowy hair pulled into a tight ponytail and seemingly always with a book in hand, she'd become not just a peaceful neighbor, but a charming friend. And one hell of a good cook. The nurse in Alana was always impressed by the healthy skin and impressive strength the petite lady had for her age. As she sat, Gayle studied her face with a concerned smile. She had a wisdom that Alana appreciated. She was about to say something when Gayle's smile dropped; her expression falling dark.

"You know, sometimes, I think I'm really going to miss days like this," Gayle said as she stared past Alana out at the street. "But you, you be sure to enjoy them for many more years. You don't have to keep taking time away from your life to check on me," she added with a chuckle.

Alana smiled. "No, it's never any trouble. Besides, someone has to bother you to keep making your famous cookies."

"Well, there's a batch in the oven right now!" She eyed Alana suspiciously above the brown rims of her glasses. "That's why you came over here, isn't it?"

They both laughed. Visits with Gayle were always like this – friendly and aloof.

A distant *ding* sounded from somewhere inside the house. The oven. "Well, speak of the devil! Cookie time, dear!" Gayle clapped her book shut and hopped up with an almost unnatural swiftness for someone in advanced years and bounded into the house. Alana could only smile and follow along.

The living room in Gayle's two-story house was as cozy as one might expect. She always kept the space perfectly tidy. A brown wool sofa with worn armrests faced a heavy wooden coffee table, which sat atop a forest green rug in front of the TV. Matching recliners with end tables bracketed each of the two windows, with an overflowing bookshelf in between. Every spot was perfect for reading. Aside from the more modern flatscreen TV, it was a living room Norman Rockwell would've envied.

Alana stepped across the room toward the old sofa, smiling as she expected the one saggy floorboard to issue its familiar creak. It delivered on cue. She plopped down while Gayle dashed through the alcove to the kitchen. She closed her eyes and inhaled the inviting aromas of warm chocolate chip cookies and fresh coffee that filled the house.

"Oh, before I forget!" Gayle spun on her heel with a dancer's grace. "How's that old green crystal I left with you? Did you ever find a spot for it?"

Perfect timing, Alana thought. She had just found a great space for it on a bookshelf that very morning. "I sure did! Right on the shelf next to one of my old art history books. It seemed fitting."

"That sounds perfect!" Gayle said. "You keep it safe, dear. Just be careful where it feels cracked. That bugger is still mighty sharp."

"Yeah, nearly cut myself on it once, but I set it with the chipped side down, so it looks brand new where it sits."

Gayle smiled big. "Good! That old rock will bring you luck, and ward off those bad spirits. Maybe even the Devil himself!"

"Oh Lord, I haven't had luck of any kind, much less any visitors since the divorce," Alana said. "Though it'd probably make sense if *El Diablo* himself showed up one night. Seems to be my taste in partners. Alana thought of her last two – no, three, failed relationships. Two were cheaters, the other one became an unapologetic liar and manipulator. She'd hoped her bad luck had run out.

Gayle raised a finger at her. "Don't tempt him, dear."

Her sudden sternness made Alana wonder, for a second, if the cracked, brick-sized green crystal really did have some kind of magic power. Old world object and all. "Don't worry. I won't."

Gayle headed toward the kitchen. Left alone on the couch, Alana aimlessly leafed through one of the magazines on the coffee table when she sensed something wrong. Suddenly, she heard a heavy buzz coming from the kitchen. Gayle groaned. Alana bolted up. "Gayle? You okay?"

When Alana entered the kitchen, she took one look and giggled like a child as Gayle stood near the sink, her teal apron pasted with the contents from her mixing bowl, which must have been set to maximum. "Filled that damned bowl too high. Be a doll and grab my other apron from the hall closet, would you? This one's a mess!"

Alana slowly turned her eyes toward the closet door in the hallway. It was as though she knew every corner of this house, what with all the times she'd helped Gayle with projects around here, including the walk-in hall closet. But something about this particular closet unsettled her, like a child afraid to go into the basement.

She stepped into the hall, trying to ignore the odd foreboding. Something about this closet always felt like cranking a Jack-in-the-Box, the monster just waiting on the other side to break out. She gripped the knob, turning it slowly at first. Once it came loose from the jamb, she swung the door open, its ancient hinges protesting with a squeal. The daylight twisted out of sight as she peered into the shadowy recess. To her unadjusted eyes, the darkness seemed to flex, as though alive. A musty waft of air shot past her and out into the hall as she quickly stepped to the center of the closet, grasping through the swirling black until her hands found the hanging string. She gave it a yank, firing the dusty old lightbulb to life. Alana couldn't believe what she saw. She remembered when Gayle could barely shut the door with all the junk nearly spilling out into the hall. But only a couple of small boxes remained, tucked toward the back wall on the floor, below a perfectly folded pair of plaid pants. They hung on a wooden rod with nothing else around them, as if on display. Gayle's green apron dangled from a coat hook on the right side wall, and as Alana reached over to grab it, her eyes were drawn back to the strange pants. Their flat brown hue with orange stripes looked even more unflattering in the dim yellow light. They were in fact, the most hideous-looking pants she'd ever seen. She wondered who'd be caught dead in these. Holding back another laugh, Alana wrinkled her nose at the now settled air as she stepped back from the dangling monstrosity. A stale, sickly-sweet smell emanated from their direction – something like Aspercreme, stale beer, and a trapped fart.

Despite the pants' unpleasantness, there was something charmingly gross about them. Like a fading ketchup stain on the seat of an old car. A story likely lurked behind every fold, every fringy wisp of fabric. Then she realized what she'd been looking at: Mr. Crabtree's old golf pants. Alana shook her head at the sight, then grabbed the apron off the hook. She turned to leave and stopped still. Gayle stood right in front of the closet door, bathed in a streaming sun beam from the window. She dropped her head down to her shoulder as an impossibly large grin spread across her face. She remained motionless, eyes stuck wide, head cocked and grinning not at Alana but past her. Into the depths of the closet.

Alana froze, with no idea what to do. She followed Gayle's eyes and looked behind her. Nothing. What was she looking at? Remembering the apron in her hand, she held it out. "Here...here's your apron Gayle. Gayle? *Gayle?*"

The charming widow blinked, then straightened up. Her wide smile faded. She glanced down at the apron and snatched it out of Alana's hands with an alarming aggressiveness.

Silent seconds ticked away.

"Are you...okay, Gayle?" Alana finally asked as she stepped out of the closet and delicately closed the door behind her, suddenly afraid to make any swift movement.

As soon as the door closed, Gayle's normal smile returned. "Thank you, dear! Come on, they came out great!" She grabbed Alana's hand and led her back into the kitchen.

Gayle scooped several cookies onto a tray. "Grab us a cup of coffee, would you?"

"The closet looks clean!" Alana offered, as she pulled a couple of mugs out of the cupboard. "Looks like you've been decluttering."

"I don't need all this junk. Can't take it with me when I go anyway."

She turned and eyed Alana a moment, sensing her curiosity, which she used to beat her to her only question. "You're probably wondering about Ted's old pants hanging in there," Gayle said, jerking a thumb toward the hall.

"I wasn't going to ask, but I definitely noticed them."

Gayle placed the cookie tray on the kitchen table, while Alana set down two cups of hot coffee as the neighbors sat. "I've kept a few knickknacks of his since he died," she shrugged. "I found those pants in the garage." She rolled her eyes across the ceiling. "Or was it the bedroom closet? At any rate, I forgot all about them. They were his favorite golf pants. 'Lucky' ones, he called them. More like *named* them, really, as if they were a pet. He'd say things like 'I'm taking Lucky to the dry cleaners!' He claimed it was because he once hit a hole-in-one while wearing them, but it always seemed like something more. They were that important to him."

She twirled a cookie in her bony fingers as a sad smile broke on her face. "I remember buying them for Ted's birthday one year, from L.L. Bean. The first mail order I ever did. That was all new back then you know. You had to find everything in a store. But then this catalog arrived one day, and I tried it out. They were so ugly, even for the time," Gayle laughed. "They were meant to be kind of a joke. But sure enough, the delivery man dropped them at the door and Ted loved them. Wore those nasty things every time he golfed. I just haven't been able to part with them."

"That's understandable. I still have things that belonged to my *abuela* inside. I think it's normal to do that, to keep some things that were important to those we've lost." Alana took a bite of fresh baked chocolate chip cookie and closed her eyes. "Amazing as always! I could eat a hundred of these." Gayle smiled as Alana took another sip of coffee. "But yeah, some stuff can be hard to part with," Alana added.

Gayle nodded. "Oh, I've tried, you know. But ever since I brought them into the house, it's like they're stuck here! I even tossed them a while ago. I seem to remember putting them into the trash one night, and the next morning, they were back!" She slapped the table for emphasis.

Alana watched her closely after that, waiting to see if her expression would shift so drastically again like she did just a minute ago. She snapped off another big chunk of cookie.

Gayle finished another coffee swig. "Maybe it was just a dream, who knows? So, I just gave up. Or maybe I'm crazy. Or that Ted's still hanging around here, I guess," she added with a soft laugh. "Oh well, sweep it under the rug, dear. Have another cookie." Despite her increasing curiosity about the grotesque pants and the strange interaction near the closet, Gayle's homemade cookies were Alana's weakness. She often thought Gayle could've had her own bakery. People would buy these by the truckload.

"What happened to Ted if I may ask? I never met him, so – "

"Died long before you were even born, dear. It's over, wow, it'll be 50 years this Friday! There was an accident. Poor Ted."

"I'm so sorry." Alana tried to offer condolences that didn't sound empty, but she didn't really know what to say.

"Mistakes happen," Gayle said with a shrug, finally biting into a cookie. "It was long ago."

Alana blinked hard. She could've never imagined such a sweet, friendly woman would be so dismissive about her husband's death, half a century in the past or not.

"But don't you worry about all that, dear. What about you? It's been a few years since the divorce." Gayle smiled. "Don't you get lonely in that house all by yourself?"

"No, I stay busy and – "

"Alana! You need another hobby than just looking after me!"

Alana rolled her eyes. "You're no hobby! "I've just…moved on and am doing my own thing now. Ever since Joelle left, I've just swept it under the rug!" she said with a little friendly mocking, and an attempt to quell Gayle's curiosity. Both ladies laughed. "Although there are times when I think I must have been born under a bad sign. Nobody else gets divorced from both a man *and* a woman."

"You're also the only person I know to move from a tropical paradise to a dump like this. Usually, it's the other way around."

Alana shrugged. "I was a child. Papa got a new job. Wasn't my choice. But do you see what I mean, Amiga? Maybe I'm cursed or something."

Gayle looked away, tapping a thumb on the table, as if in thought. "Curses! What good are they?" Gayle looked directly at Alana. "Besides dear, people like you don't get cursed. They get *chosen*."

Alana straightened; a trace of worry flashed in her eyes. "Chosen for what?"

"You're special, dear." Gayle folded her napkin into a tiny square. "It will all make sense soon, you'll see."

Alana assumed she was just being polite and supportive, but something about Gayle's serious tone made her want to change the subject. She looked around the kitchen, stalling as best she could. "So, what about this place?" Hasn't it been lonely since Ted – "

Gayle silenced her with a wave of her hand. "It was our home and I'm going to keep it our home. Like those old pants, I suppose. If something of Ted's is still here, then *he's* still here."

~ * ~

Later that night, Alana sat in her favorite, her only, recliner, trying to read. But she couldn't get her question about Ted out of her mind. She was so astonished at how quickly Gayle brushed it off; it was really unlike her. She flipped on the TV, hoping for a distraction. The third channel yielded a *Golden Girls* rerun, which reminded her instantly of Gayle and their conversation. Her mind ran back over the relaxing-turned-bizarre afternoon all over again, so she decided to give in and do a little googling to see if she could find any information on what happened to old Ted Crabtree. She was excited to find the local newspaper archived all the obituaries dating back more than a century, then crestfallen to see it was behind a paywall. She felt hesitant to pay for it, even if it only cost two bucks.

The next morning, Alana drove to the downtown library to examine the microfilm from the year and month of Ted's death. She was sure to find his obituary that way. After about ten minutes of scrolling, she found it. Her heart raced. She wasn't shocked when she read the words "mysterious circumstances" in the copy. In fact, they may as well have been written in flashing neon lights. She nodded with validation. She scrolled the microfilm dates back a week and found one short article about the investigation into the death of Ted Crabtree. The article explained his death was sudden, after he became violently ill while working his normal shift as a security guard at Oakville Bank & Trust. No evidence of foul play. No present disease. He simply…died. And that strengthened Alana's suspicions even further. As she researched Ted's mysterious demise, she kept thinking of Gayle's remark from yesterday: "mistakes happen."

The next couple of weeks passed normally and Alana worried less about Gayle's behavior that day, or if it had any connection with her asking about her late husband. Maybe she wasn't feeling well or was having a spike in anxiety – Alana could relate to that much, at least.

The two neighbors spent Thanksgiving at Alana's house along with a few friends who had no familial obligations that day. It was perfect, Alana thought. The small group laughed, watched football, and sipped cocktails over a simple spread of turkey sandwiches and a makeshift salad bar. Gayle supplied an economy-sized batch of her famous cookies for dessert. As she walked her elderly friend home at evening's end, Alana offered to help put up her Christmas decorations, which Gayle gladly accepted.

The morning after Thanksgiving was bright and cool, but the sun still promised a twinge of warmth, making for a nice day for outside work. Thermos in hand, Alana made her way across to Gayle's house where she had already begun sliding boxes out of the garage. She was particularly excited about starting with her newest piece of exterior décor – a large, lighted wreath with a giant red bow on the front. It was comically large for the front door, and nobody would see it on the side of the house. So, the ladies agreed it would look best and fit perfectly on the sliver of wall just above the front porch. The only snag was that the space was a full two stories up.

Alana ran back home to grab her ex-husband's old aluminum extension ladder to hang the wreath. Gayle stood in the yard below, ready to help eyeball the precise spot to hang the ornamentation.

"We really don't have to do this, you know," Gayle said. "It can just hang off the porch instead of above it."

"No," Alana insisted. "I can get it up there. It'll be perfect." Alana was always willing to help, especially if it meant she could show off some of her handy skills. It made her feel more useful. She leaned the beat up old ladder that her former husband used on jobs for his construction company against the wall next to the porch. Once it was steady enough, she climbed up to gauge the height and position for the wreath.

"Higher dear, Gayle said. She pointed to an area just above where Alana stood. "I think it should go right up there between those two windows, not below them."

"Okay, then I need to come down and extend this thing." Alana had no fear of heights, or working from a ladder, since she used to do some side work for her brother painting houses. With her then-husband in construction, the dream of a family house flipping business was conceived, but then put to rest with the divorce. She extended the second set of rungs and repositioned the ladder to the height Gayle wanted. Alana stepped back on, going slow to steady herself. Each step felt higher than she originally thought. Though only two stories up where she stood, it was actually more than three down to the flagstone walkway at the bottom of the short berm the house stood upon. Alana reached the area in between the second-story windows and placed a hand on the wall near where she figured Gayle might want the wreath. "How's this right here?" she shouted.

No answer came.

She studied the exterior wall, testing perfectly centered locations, feeling around for the right spot in the mortar to set the wreath's anchor. But a stillness fell upon her. The realization that Gayle never answered blinded her, like turning the lights on in a darkened room. Her pulse hammered in her ears. The ladder wobbled as if on uneven ground. Alana looked back over her shoulder toward the empty yard, careful not to completely turn around or she'd risk a misstep and lose her balance.

"Gayle? Gayle? You alright?" Anxiousness swirled in her gut like poison. Something was wrong.

Alana grasped the ladder firmly. She took a slow, measured first step down before she could descend as quickly as possible to make sure Gayle was okay. Before she landed on the next rung down, the window just to her right shot open. Before Alana could react, Gayle reached her wiry arm out and gave the ladder a strong shove. Alana frantically grabbed at the wall but only got a handful of air.

~ * ~

Beep…beep…beep…

The soft, pulsing sound was faint and distant, going off at the same interval. Soon the clatter of overlapping voices joined the subtle noise. The darkness began to lighten, dissolving into an unfocused swirl of light. Alana tried to blink her disorientation away, unaware of her surroundings. She brushed her hand across a thick, damp fabric wrapped around her throbbing head. A sharp pang of pain ran along the base of her neck – which was held immobile by some heavy, metallic device. Then her bloodshot eyes widened with remembrance. The house. The ladder. Gayle.

Alana tried to speak but only a pitiful, raspy whisper escaped from her throat. "Gayle!" She struggled to sit up and managed to move almost an inch before giving up.

"Take it easy, sweetie, you've had a nasty fall," a blonde woman in blue scrubs and a lab coat said.

"Sh…she tried to kill me!"

"I'm Doctor Rosenbloom. This is Detective Mike Novak," she said, gesturing to the man behind her. "You've been here almost five days. You fell into a mild coma but came out of it early this morning. You've suffered a small fracture to your skull, damaged some ligaments in your neck, and you have broken your collarbone. Another inch or two, and you might not have made it. You landed at a lucky angle. And you have really good muscular tone and density," she added with a smile. "Athlete?"

"Volleyball. It hurts…my…," Alana winced and closed her eyes.

The doctor put a reassuring hand on Alana's forearm. "I know, honey, we'll take care of that. Believe it or not, the pain is a good sign. You're going to be okay, but you need to rest here awhile. We've notified your family, they are outside. I'll go get them."

As the doctor left the room, the man stepped toward the bed, holding out his badge. A wasted professional gesture since Alana couldn't make it out. She couldn't have cared less anyway.

"Mrs. Aldridge, I'm so sorry to –"

"Reyes," Alana whispered. "My maiden name."

"Understood, Ms. Reyes, pardon me," Novak said. "I hate to trouble you right now, I know you need to rest, so I'll be very quick. I just have to ask you what you remember."

Alana felt so foggy, unsure where to start. She glanced about the drab hospital room. Her vision was in better focus. A banking commercial was on the wall-mounted TV. The blinds were shut. She didn't know what time of day it was – or what *day* it was. Then it hit her: Gayle's wreath.

"Gayle. I was on the ladder at her house, helping her hang a wreath, and she– "Alana paused to collect herself. It hurt to speak. "She opened the window…"

The detective nodded. "Yes. Some kids were out playing down the street and saw you fall. Their parents called the paramedics. They found you unconscious on the sidewalk, and Mrs. Crabtree dead in the living room. That's when they called us in."

"Dead? How?"

"Given her age it could've been natural causes, we're still waiting on the autopsy report. But under the circumstances we're investigating everything."

"She was elderly but…so energetic," Alana said.

"That's why we're looking into it," the detective said. "With what happened to you at the same time, it's even more strange to find her how we did."

"What do you mean?"

"Mrs. Ald – I'm sorry, Ms. Reyes, you should rest. I think I have what I need for now, thank you."

"Please. What manner?" Alana insisted.

Detective Novak took a deep breath. "She was lying with her eyes and mouth wide open, like an apparent shock. She held a large kitchen knife in one hand, and we found this in her other," he pulled a small plastic evidence bag from his briefcase and handed it to Alana. She nearly gasped in surprise.

"I lost this watch months ago! How did she get this?"

"We were hoping you could tell us. Were you close? Had she been known to take things without knowing? Lack of awareness? Memory troubles? Or signs of dementia that you know of?"

"We were pretty close," Alana admitted. "I don't know how often she took things. But she kept some things, stuff that belonged to her husband that she couldn't get rid of."

"Mm hmm," the detective muttered as he tapped on his cell phone a few times. There was a soft knock on the door, Alana's brother and sister. Detective Novak held up a finger, asking them for another minute. "That's not all. We found Mrs. Crabtree on the floor, right on top of a loose floor plank. It turns out there were several loose planks in a row, like they were made to be removeable. They all ran right under her living room rug. We lifted them and found some old coins and jewelry inside under the subfloor." He pulled a small notepad from his coat pocket and flipped it to a page. "Along with Ted Crabtree's wallet, his wedding ring, two shards of some kind of green glass, and a photograph of you."

"What? What for? I couldn't imagine why she'd have that. And hide it no less."

Detective Novak paced to the side of Alana's bed and looked right into her green, bloodshot eyes. "Well, that's one of the things we are trying to find out," he said. "One last thing. Did Mrs. Crabtree have any superstitions that you know about? Maybe a lucky number? Inferences to certain objects?"

Alana looked down for a moment in thought. "Not that I know of, why?"

"She seemed to have some kind of obsession with the number three. The number was scrawled on the back of the loose floor planks. Even on the joists below. She had three of each of the same type of coin. Three crucifixes. Three rings. A deck of cards – all of them threes of hearts and diamonds." He thumbed at his phone screen a few times, then gave it a tap, and held it in front of Alana. "And an old bible with the words, 'Three Chimes. A quiet end for those who know,' written in red marker. Written three times on every third page. Any idea what any of that could mean?"

Alana stared ahead, unknowing what to say. The commercials on the TV changed back to the airing of *It's a Wonderful Life*.

~*~

The Watcher of King's Cross

Yesterday was the anniversary.

Has it really been thirty-five years? So much has changed. *Always too busy*, General Kevin Hollister thought. That was his crutch. Bury yourself in work, and you can avoid other things. It always worked for him – he wouldn't have made it this far if it hadn't.

He leaned against the frame of the floor-to-ceiling window in his suite-level office, gazing down at the streets of the new Chicago. The cars and people were barely visible from his view on the 110th floor. He sighed, catching himself thinking once again about whether or not to go. He liked the old Chicago better, even with all its corruption, violence, and widespread crime.

Being a chief executive at Cygnvs afforded him almost everything someone could dream about in life: wealth, power, freedom, control, safety, even a sliver of fame. But even with those earthly riches, he realized the corporation's arcane practices and sinister, world domineering mission cost him every ounce of contentment – the one thing he sought the most. He had that once. At least until that night thirty-five years ago.

With the world spiraling toward chaos – the very thing Cygnvs sought to simultaneously create and control – Hollister felt an undeniable pull to just leave. He no longer cared what the rest of the top brass were doing at HQ in Romania. Hell, it was a world away. This was something he didn't need to explain. He hadn't been to the gravesite since the funeral.

The general scanned the horizon. Something in the sunset beckoned him. Before he could change his mind again, he hustled over to his large marble desk and typed a hasty email to his understudies, notifying them he'd be out of town for a few days. He grabbed his cell phone off the desk and paused, noting the notification for the six new texts that awaited him. He ignored those, but he did remember there was one message he needed to send. He scrolled to Walter Sherman's contact.

Hey Sherm! Hope all is well in NC! I'm finally going to listen to you. Heading to Harland Falls tomorrow.

He pocketed the phone, stuffed a few papers and his iPad into his work bag, snatched his keys and coat and headed for the door. The buzzing in his pocket stopped him as he flipped off his office lights. With a sad smile, he retrieved his phone, anticipating Walter's reply text.

About time. I know he'd appreciate it. Safe travels.

The general stepped into the hallway, closing the hand-carved oaken office door behind him. The fancy electronic lock engaged with a *snap* and a *beep* as he headed down the hall to the elevator.

He walked slowly. Hollister was a calculating man, never letting impulse overtake analysis. If he had thoughts, he needed to organize them before they vanished. As he neared the elevator, he wondered if he should just go up there immediately, with no more delays. He also thought that the obsidian marble floors and walls in this building were a bit much.

With all the resources at his fingertips – including his choice from a fleet of corporate jets – he could make the journey from Chicago to Harland Falls, Minnesota, quicker than anyone. But the guilt over not visiting the cemetery returned in a heavy wave, and he realized the need to do this right. And do it alone.

The general woke at 4 o'clock, far earlier than normal, and set to work preparing for his trip. Through a carefully orchestrated sequence of more officially crafted emails, some sneaky GPS augmentation that few Cygnvs operatives knew how to implement, and a couple falsified itineraries for good measure, he was satisfied that he succeeded in misdirecting his own security entourage. He could hit the road by himself, before anyone arrived at the office that day, in peace.

~ * ~

6:26 A.M.

The rising sun hung mercifully in his blind spot as he headed northwest, affording him a daybreak-clear view of the wooded hillsides and rolling Midwestern expanse. Though he was anxious to visit the cemetery, he tried not to rush to get there. Just driving made Hollister feel more in touch with the world; more normal. More human.

He loved seeing the fields at dawn. The sun, still low on the horizon behind him, bathed the autumn browns and yellows in thick tangerine light. For a moment, he had forgotten what he was there to do. It felt like he'd arrived in another world; one so different, so *normal*, compared to the terrifying one he lived in – that he'd even helped create – every day. He eased his new Chevy Tahoe along the highway, the mesmerizing hum of the engine and whooshing roadway noise lulling him to a sense of relaxation he hadn't felt in years. Just north of Madison, Wisconsin, Hollister's phone rang. Very few people would call his personal cell at this time of day. He didn't bother to look at the number on the screen. *Shit, work.* He let it ring several times before finally slapping the answer button on the steering wheel as he took a deep breath. "Hollister."

"Hey, kid. Wake you up?" He instantly recognized the gruff voice on the other end. A relief washed over him.

"Sherm! Thank God," he exhaled. "No, not at all! Been on the road a while now. Just passed the Dells. I'll be up there today. How about you? Sitting on the beach over there?"

"Not yet," he said. Hollister could practically hear him smile. "But probably later."

Hollister stared out at the horizon during the lengthy ensuing silence, unsure what to say next. Fortunately for him, Walter beat him to it. "Listen, since you're going, there's something I need to tell you. About that night. Something that's been bothering me for…a long time."

He straightened in his driver's seat, preparing for some news he wasn't going to like. "Okay, go on."

As Hollister heard Walter's words, his mind drifted back to the events that claimed his father's life. It still all felt so empty, so worthless to him. He thought of that last day, how it all happened, remembering every detail he was told as though he'd witnessed it himself.

Dad, that is, Lieutenant Roland Hollister, stalwart veteran of the Harland Falls P.D. in northeastern Minnesota, shouldn't have been on the scene that day.

Driving home early one morning after working another double shift, the dispatch call alerted Dad and his partner, Walter Sherman, to an armed, residential robbery in-progress in a neighborhood only a block from their location. The two exhausted officers sped to the scene, ready to assist. Dad bolted out of the car, drawing his sidearm as he inched toward the front door of the house with Walter covering him a few paces behind.

The front door stood partially ajar, broken through the frame as if kicked in. The two officers flanked the entrance, announcing their presence with official and stern warnings. There was no response, but they could hear movement inside. With a nod to his partner, Dad reached for the open door. Walter realized the danger of the potential ambush too late. Just as he called out for him to wait, the thief's bullet struck Dad in the neck. He stumbled backward into Walter, blood gushing from the wound. Walter dragged his friend, gasping through crimson-coated bubbles for air, off the porch to relative safety in the yard. By the time he charged back into the house to return fire, the suspect had fled. They found the owner of the house, an elderly woman named Gladys, hiding in an upstairs closet, clutching a cordless phone. Dad lay dead on the front lawn.

In the months after, young Kevin Hollister only knew he had to be strong for his family – that's what would've been expected of him. Plus, what could he have really done? He was too young and didn't know who to turn to. He wanted to scream. But he'd never lash out against God or blame Him. Instead, he withdrew. He wrote. In private. He didn't even know what it was until much later. Journaling? A diary? No, girls did that kind of thing, or so the TV would have him believe. What he did was different. Stronger. Colder. And it helped.

A distant voice called to him back from the memory.

"You there, Kev? Hello? Hello?"

Snapping back to the phone call, he realized he'd spaced out. *A dangerous thing to do on the highway, Kev.* It was an uncharacteristic lapse of concentration; one he was sure he'd almost enjoy berating himself for. He took his foot off the gas pedal when he saw the digital speedometer read 98. "Yeah, sorry...sorry. "

He took a deep breath and relaxed his grip on the steering wheel. "It's okay Walter, really. It wasn't your fault. You shouldn't live with that."

"I've lived with it since that day because I should've known better than to let him go in there first, kid. He'd just worked a double – maybe a triple, who knows. I was on that same long shift. We were both exhausted, but he looked more ragged than me by a longshot. I may have been tired, but he was burned out. Your dad was always working. Even when he was off duty, he was on duty, know what I mean?"

Hollister never thought about it quite like that, but it made sense to him. *Dad had a fierce dedication to his job. He believed if he let his guard down even an inch, he'd never be able to put it back up. He placed immense pressure on himself to maintain our family's livelihood.*

As a result, Kevin Hollister spent more time alone growing up than a vibrant, curious child should. He had friends, but dad was a real hero. Hollister's youth was filled with constant reminders by his mother that dad had an important job; he saved people.

Looking back, the general realized it was probably not the best way to raise a family, but what did he know? He never wanted that for himself, so who is he to judge? His dad, the ever-steady lieutenant, knew no other way to be. In a sense, he was proud of his father for that.

"He was fatigued that morning whether he'd admit it or not," Walter said. "But I wasn't thinking straight. I should've taken the lead! I should've noticed the way the door was obscuring the room behind it sooner. Even *one second* sooner. It was reckless on my part, kid. I was too slow. Guess I was more tired than I realized that day. I'm sorr—"

"And even if you did say anything, he would've argued, and you both would've wasted precious time!" The asphalt turned rough and uneven under his wheels. Hollister turned up the volume on the call. "You were partners for more than 15 years. You of all people knew how stubborn he could be. He always trusted you. There's nothing to forgive."

There was another long pause.

Walter let out a deep sigh, taking three and a half decades of guilt along with it. "Thank you, Kev. You know, I've kept that inside for thirty-five years. I wasn't sure when or even how I could tell you. Maybe I was waiting for you to go back there. I never wanted you to blame me, but I didn't want you to think I was speaking badly of your father either. He was more than a great cop. He was a damned fine man. I'm sorry I wasn't a better partner that day."

Nausea and adrenaline wrestled for dominance of the general's insides. He knew the details of what happened but had no idea Walter, who became a father figure to him in the aftermath, carried this burden for so long. He'd hoped he had just purged himself of it for good.

~*~

Traffic had increased significantly on the highway as the morning wore on. Hollister felt a new anxiousness creep up on him – beyond just his nerves about making the trip. After hearing Walter's story, the yearning, the sheer pull to Harland Falls, gained strength. He was supposed to be there. He felt it. He just didn't know *why*. It was almost like the other feeling he often experienced – an intense Déjà vu, like thinking of an old movie he hadn't seen or a song he hadn't heard in some time, and then it would suddenly be on. Or how he'd think of an old acquaintance and then he'd hear from that person within a day. Or the countless times where he could tell exactly what someone was going to say moments before they did. He didn't know what all of that meant. A therapist once told him he was likely clairvoyant – or was it clairsentient? One of the 'clair's' at any rate, but he'd always shooed it off out of fear that trying to understand what it really was would make him crazy. But the closer he got to Minnesota, he felt that vibe again, gaining in intensity, connecting to some obscure energy that felt like it was trying to prove to him that he was doing the right thing.

Hollister caught himself once again on the precipice of overthinking. In an attempt to shake it off, he flipped on the radio just as the opening beat of "Take the Money and Run" filled his truck's cabin. "Breakdown" followed. By the time "You're No Good" came on, he could barely feel the tires on the road, no longer dwelling about what he was doing there in the first place. It was just him, the music and the serenity of the upper Midwest. As the road to Minnesota stretched on before him, he cracked an unforced smile for the first time in months.

~*~

Ominous clouds swept over the area and replaced the earlier bright sun, drenching King's Cross Abbey in picturesque grayscale.

He parked his truck in front of the property and walked up to the dilapidated iron gates. They stood open, one side listing hopelessly on rusty hinges as if it would fall to the ground any second. The place looked smaller than he remembered. And old. Abandoned. Thick grass and patches of weeds showed that landscape maintenance was apparently no longer a priority. Far off to his right, the charred remains of the old church sat on the hill overlooking the forgotten graves. Hollister stepped through the gates and walked straight toward row six, plot three – the exact location forever etched into his mind. Even if he didn't remember the number, it wouldn't be hard to find.

Roland's ornate grave stood out in stark contrast against the rest of the pale gray stone slabs that dotted the yard. And it should. He was well-known and well-liked. A local hero. The black marble headstone stood almost as tall as the general, inlaid with silver granite accents and golden lettering. The epitaph practically gleamed through the misty gloom.

LT. ROLAND JACEK HOLLISTER
1941-1988
BELOVED PROTECTOR OF PEACE

It was then that General Hollister realized he had a problem: he didn't know what to do.

At first, it didn't feel quite real to stand there again after all these years. He'd long outgrown the benefit of youth and whatever level of innate ignorance that provided. But knowing his father's remains were resting just six feet below where he stood in this rotted, overgrown cemetery seemed...all wrong to him. But also, familiar. And that's what troubled him the most. He stared at the grave as he stood rock still, unmoving, in a sort of reverie.

Suddenly he felt lighter. Freer. A calmness descended upon him, one that he welcomed gratefully. It was like a penance, one he didn't even have to make, but had been accepted. Above, the gray skies thickened, threatening rain. The breeze carried with it the telltale northern chill, its sharpness heralding the coming winter. The general wasn't sure how long he would remain. How long *should* he remain? He brushed his jacket open, casually placing both hands in his pockets. He grasped a handful of keys and rocked back on his heels.

"Your father," a deep voice next to him said.

Hollister snapped a look to his left, nearly stumbling off balance, surprised by the sudden appearance of the stranger. Where did he come from? He was completely alone just a moment before...wasn't he?

"Where did – I'm sorry?"

A tall, gray-haired man stood before him. He nodded toward the headstone behind the general. "Here. Your father." He spoke slowly and calculating, as if he were concerned someone was listening. He took a step – more like a glide – toward the general.

"Yes...um, pardon me, do I know you?" the general asked. He paused and looked at his father's grave. "Did you know *him?*"

As Hollister watched the man shift his golden eyes toward the headstone, he instinctively – and inconspicuously – slid his right hand from his pants pocket to rest on his sidearm, concealed by the low waistline of his jacket. He looked around the barren graveyard. Nobody else was there. He'd made sure of it.

Hollister returned his attention to the stranger, giving him a long look while awaiting his answer. The man stood well over six feet tall, wearing a black raincoat buttoned tightly around him. His sharp but handsome features made his age unclear, though his snowy hair, tied in a tight ponytail, betrayed the fact he must have some years on him. "Well," he began. "Not exactly. But I know *of* him. I've been around these parts a time or two. You tend to remember the important people in a place like this."

"Are you from Harland Falls? Or do you have family here?"

The stranger raised an eyebrow and smiled, as if amused by the question. "I'm from...elsewhere," he said. "I have family everywhere you might say. But I've been a regular visitor here over the years. This place is special."

Hollister scanned the decrepit old cemetery again and finally fixed his gaze upon the crumbling ruins of the church. Much of it was still intact, though heavily burned out and broken, as if a bomb exploded right in the center of it. The wrecked frame sat twisted at a sharp angle; the bell tower practically leaned over the hill.

"Maybe it was once," Hollister shrugged, hoping this conversation would lighten. "But ever since the murders and the church up there being destroyed, old Harland is like a ghost town these days, even with the redevelopment going on." He looked toward the church again. "At least they decided not to touch this place. I think it's an important reminder of—"

"Ghosts," the tall man mused, cutting Hollister off. "They always seem to be part of the story, don't they?" He laughed to himself. "Just because we can't see them, doesn't mean they aren't there. Just because we can't talk to them, doesn't mean they don't listen." The wind picked up, whipping the back of the general's neck. Leaves tumbled across the unkempt grass, swirling atop the gravestones like a miniature tornado. Hollister watched the phenomenon, grateful for the short distraction.

"I suppose," the general said. He felt like this was finally going somewhere.

"You were young when it happened," the stranger said matter-of-factly.

Just what Hollister thought. He nodded. "Nine."

The man stepped even closer to the general. He lowered his voice further, nearly whispering. "Such a shame. Such a burden that must have been for so young a child to bear."

"I managed," Hollister shrugged. "Didn't have much of a choice. Just had to deal with things and grow up. So may I ask again, who are you?"

Just as he opened his mouth to speak, he flicked his eyes at the church ruins. "My apologies," he told the general. "Thought I saw a ghost of my own up there."

Hollister rolled his eyes.

"You remained strong for your family, did well in school, stayed clear of the troubles most youth get themselves into. And you obviously became successful."

Who was this man and how did he know these things? Hollister felt at a disadvantage. He shifted his feet for a stronger stance and faced him. "Okay, forgive me, but *who are you?*" The stranger ignored him, and just kept looking past him at Roland's headstone. Hollister gritted his teeth so hard his jaw went numb. "Look at me!"

The gray haired man faced him as commanded, squinting his flaxen-irised eyes as if in annoyance. "I don't think I appreciate your tone."

Hollister fingered the snap on his holster. Given his position with Cygnvs and a face made far too public for his liking, he wasn't taking any chances. "My tone? You're intruding on my personal business with what seems like some kind of axe to grind with me. I have no idea who you are but apparently you know all about me. So, you can deal with my fucking tone while you— "

"You!" the tall stranger barked. "You, a nine-year-old child, in shock from your father's murder. You wanted to scream, to find the man who did it and execute justice – or payback – as you once believed. Yet you were raised in the Church, so loyal and unwaveringly devout, even at such a young age. Never would you *dare* to blame Him!" He lowered his voice to the raspy whisper again. "So, you blamed someone else, didn't you?"

"One last time, sir!" Hollister snapped the strap off his holster, ready to draw his weapon. *"Who are you?"*

"Something is happening up there." The man jerked a thumb over toward the church. He scanned the sky as he spoke. "There's a hatred about, a silent scream. *He* will notice." He took another step toward Hollister, standing so close they could've embraced. "Like you. You know about silence, don't you? After all, it was in secret that you wrote all those letters."

Hollister went numb. Bile and embarrassment surged in his throat. He took an unbalanced step back from the man.

"Hate mail in fact. They were noticed, as well. You lashed out in the only way you knew, blaming and threatening the one you believed was responsible for your father's death. Truly impressive, to be honest. A strong but misguided child with such aggressive prose."

Hollister stood in stunned silence. He never told *anyone* about the hateful letters he had written. Why would he? It all seemed so silly now, almost forty years later. Nothing more than a child's imagination running wild. But the stranger was right. He was blaming someone with each word he wrote, but he knew he had no real recipient, no place to actually send those letters. So, every time he finished one, he'd tear it up into tiny pieces, throwing the shredded paper away in small clusters in different trash cans to make sure his mother would never find them. He dreaded the thought of what would happen if a churchgoing, God-fearing woman like Judith Hollister discovered her only son was writing violent letters to Satan.

He took another step back, ready to draw his sidearm just as the man smiled at him with both hands raised. The stranger offered a polite nod, signaling his compliance. Palms still up, he began to walk away.

The general sighed and snapped his holster strap shut. After a few steps, the man stopped and turned to face Hollister. "You know," he said. I've waited for many of your years for the right moment to thank you. No other form of worship was ever so touching."

This couldn't be happening, Hollister thought.

The man looked skyward again. "Your chastisement is coming, General. But you already knew that didn't you? Underneath your self-absorbed Cygnvs collar you're still that same faithful nine-year-old child, praying for peace. Just a victim of circumstance, yes?"

Hollister opened his mouth to speak, but the man flicked a finger toward the sky, silencing him.

"It's okay, General. *He* knows."

The man turned away one final time, stalking off toward the hills. "He always knows."

~ * ~

Ora Pro Nobis

March 11

I was too late.

The morning sun broke right at 6:12, giving the snow-covered yard outside the old stone church a fiery sheen. In the tower high above, the massive bell tolled for the third time in the minute preceding the frozen dawn. The fading peal of the heavy, final chime hung in the air as I approached. The sound was joined by voices – an echo of distant screams. The area smelled of ice and decay. The sunrise appeared as wrong as was foretold – faded, partially veiled in the growing azure blur. Dark, scattered clouds drifted past it as if coasting downhill. The sky looked tired.

And it was burning.

His sign, like that of a blazing teardrop, appeared high above the sun to the northeast, partially obscured by its morning glare.

Sirens wailed in the distance, growing louder as the local onlookers drifted out of their homes from the neighborhood across the road like some wandering herd of animals. The confused response of people at bloody scenes never ceased to both amaze and revile me.

I kept at a distance slightly downhill from the arriving throng of police and medical personnel to observe in relative obscurity. I had no desire to entertain their suspicions, and I needed to find the one who was in charge. Dozens of men and women darted about, taking pictures, and cordoning off the area to keep the neighborly group away. So, I waited and watched.

She had long, black hair, tied back away from her caramel face. She walked slower than the rest. More contemplative. She spoke steadily into her cell phone. Calm. Dictating. The woman appeared to give orders and pointed her staff toward different areas of the property. Then she walked to the barricaded line to address the group of local people who'd gathered at the edge of the yard. It looked like a sermon.

As she left the crowd, I walked across the still-frozen yard toward the church. She spun toward me with the sharp movements of a well-trained soldier.

"Sir? Don't move!"

We eyed one another closely as I approached. I kept my palms up in a display of peace. She rested one hand inside her coat and pocketed her phone with the other. I had one chance to convince her I meant no harm, that I was one of *them*. "Apologies ma'am. I heard some commotion coming from this way. I'm here on official parish business." I presented her with my identification before she demanded it. She chewed at her top lip as she stared at the badge.

"How could the church send an official investigator so quickly?" she asked, cocking her eyebrow as she handed the ID badge back to me.

"Under normal circumstances they couldn't, of course. I was already in the area. I've been investigating several parishes in the state, in fact."

She regarded me with keen, hazel eyes. "Uh huh. I'm Lieutenant Erin Soto." We shook hands. "And as you can see, Mr. Harrison, this is a very fresh crime scene, and we have to be careful. Would you mind standing out by the lot for a bit? I'd like to talk with you more, but I need to get some things done here immediately. You understand."

"I'll be here," I told her as I headed to the small parking lot. There was a bench near a monument of Saint Matthew. I contemplated going against her wishes and going up the tower to see it for myself. I felt near to my charge now, and that meant I was close to finishing the job. Waiting only tested what little patience I had left. But I needed to not arouse further suspicion. So, I did what I seemed to do best. I observed. Again.

The impressive old church looked majestic in the morning light, perched atop a short hill, overlooking a field of graves. Church towers have played an important role in religion for centuries. More than just a call to prayer or the signal for celebration, many steeples across the world have become something of a cornerstone of parishioners' faith. St. Michael's was an imposing structure, made entirely of gray stone with intricate, hand-chiseled archways and ornate statuary, built when people here took pride in architecture. Atop the nave roof, four smaller buttresses jutted out from narrow pinnacles to support the tallest, main tower where the old bell now hung dormant. Something felt wrong in this place. Different than what I expected; misaligned with the foretelling.

Nearly thirty minutes passed before I spotted Lieutenant Soto walking out of the church. I stood to greet her as she approached me.

"Thanks for sticking around," she said. "Listen. I called the parish office when I was inside. They haven't heard of Zachary Harrison. Want to try again, bud?"

She stood cross-armed and still between me and the church. Her officers milled about, and the throng of neighbors stood as before, in a tight group along the makeshift fence behind me, as if the detective and I were onstage in some production for their entertainment. Lieutenant Soto glared at me. I couldn't blame her for her disbelief. "My orders come from much higher up, detective. They probably just haven't notified the local office yet that I'm here. You've seen my identification. I promise you my credentials will check out. Would I have waited here, otherwise?"

She pointed a finger at me. "I sure hope you're who you say you are. I'm going on the assumption your ID is legit, and believe me, I'll be following up on that closely. But frankly, I'm impatient. So, for right now, please level with me. Off the record, if you want. This whole day is fucked up enough anyway. I want to know who you are, what you're doing here, how you happened to avoid this massacre, and what specifically interests you in this church?"

"That all sounds rather *on* the record to me, detective."

She took off her sunglasses and rubbed her bloodshot hazel eyes. This one was different, I realized. She seemed to care and trusted her intuition. The way she secured the scene and how her fellow officers followed her orders closely showed she was assertive. Direct. A leader. I could've gone up to the tower and got what I needed myself. But I became genuinely curious to hear what she would say next. She sat down on the bench, zipping up her blue, official-looking jacket against the cold morning breeze. The wind tousled her hair; a shiny strand fell across her face as she sighed and peered in the distance.

"I grew up here," she said. "It's nice, you know? A nice town. Good people who are always willing to help each other. Sure, there's problems and crime like any other town, but we do our best to keep it to a minimum. That's why this is so strange, so unlike this place. No forced entry. No damage to the building. No weapons or bullet casings. Probably no prints either once they finish dusting. And yet, I have nineteen dead people dead in there. They just showed up for early morning mass and their heads caved in. No witnesses either of course, except for your random appearance." She pointed to the sky. "And for whatever goddamned reason the fucking sun rose in the *north*!"

I looked up at it with anxious wonder, as if the sight would change. I wanted to explain that I knew it was going to happen; what it all meant. But I couldn't tell her anything that would make sense to her. Before I could try, she again looked right into my eyes.

"But you said you heard something?"

"Shouting voices, like a celebration," I said. "And the church bell rang. That's it."

She raised an eyebrow. "So, the congregation was alive when you got here?"

I shook my head. "I don't know. I never went inside. They were as you found them." I gestured back toward the road. "I heard the noise from a distance."

"Then who did these voices belong to? The only people awake at the time were the early mass attendees, and why would they be shouting? Could you even hear them from the outside? You either somehow did, or you don't know what it was that you heard. So, level with me. You are—"

I raised my hand. "You already know, lieutenant, I am an investigator. My home office is in Rome – I was going to tell you earlier that my orders come from well above the local church. I've been sent to this parish to look into—," I wasn't sure what to say. I could only look behind the detective for a moment as I gathered a reason for my being here. "Theft. There have been a number of robberies or other misplacements of valuable items from several parishes across the Midwest. I'm seeing if there's a connection, and of course to attempt to recover the missing or stolen items."

"Nobody has reported any theft from any church around here to my knowledge," she said. "This is a small town, *Zachary*. We'd know about that."

"If objects of high material or intrinsic value to a church become damaged or go missing, they are reported and investigated internally first, based on their importance. It may seem…counterproductive to do it that way to you, but policy states to involve the authorities second, in certain cases. This is one of them."

She stared at me for another long moment. Her brow furrowed; lips pursed. "Tell me then, what was taken from here?" Her incredulity was palpable.

"Here? Nothing taken. Something *received*." I pointed up toward the bell tower.

She looked up at the tower. "What? The bell? Yeah, they got a new one installed a couple weeks ago. Pretty big scene actually. Violent. I'm sure you've heard if you've been in the area. As I said, small town."

"Anything else?" I pressed.

"Well, I'm not sure how important this is, but in addition to all the chaos, apparently the bell didn't work. Missing parts or something. They're still trying to fix it. I used to attend this church, so I thought it was a little odd they'd go through all the trouble to hoist a huge bell all the way up there if it didn't work. But people in the neighborhood – and you – said they heard it ring this morning. Not like a normal bell for service though. Just two or three random chimes, apparently."

"And?"

Lieutenant Soto shrugged. "Some of them said they sounded different. Like the rings were heavier. Longer. With an echo, like it created a sound wave, like you described. I thought that was because of whatever parts they were missing, maybe it didn't sound like it's supposed to."

I nodded, my suspicions feeling confirmed. "That is why I've arrived, Lieutenant."

"To look at the bell up there?" she asked. "Why? Was it stolen from somewhere?"

"Yes, actually. But mostly because I think I know what that bell does."

~ * ~

Eleven days past.

Dozens of townspeople gathered around the fenced-off construction area at the church, watching with impressed curiosity as a construction crew prepared to lift the ancient-looking bell from a flatbed trailer, and raise it up into its resting place.

Workers in the tower monitored the heavy-duty winch as it pulled the slack on the two inch thick, aircraft-quality steel cables connected to tabs on the bell canons. After seeing the sheer size of the bell when it arrived the previous day, the crew removed the tower windows and surrounding supports, and still had to notch the lower façade of the spire to wedge it in. Concerned murmurs spread through the line of onlookers as the pitted, dark bronze bell rose off the trailer bed. It was big – too big, it seemed, even for the imposing 200-foot tall stone tower at St. Michael's. Suddenly, a woman's frantic voice shot out from the crowd. "Stop working! Drop it! Drop it!"

Everyone turned to look at the thin, disheveled woman as she stumbled through the crowd toward the construction workers. She looked like she had slept on a mound of mud. Frayed, graying hair spilled down over a ragged brown jacket. She stared at the bell and pointed. Her eyes were wild, bloodshot rings around dilated pupils and damp with tears.

"Drop it where it is! You must *not* hang this thing!"

The crowd parted around her. The lady paid no attention to them, her attention was on the bell. Nobody knew what to do. Several minutes passed while the woman, with closed eyes, whispered to herself as if in prayer.

"Excuse me, miss?" a man from the crowd said.

"Hon? Are you okay?" the woman next to him added.

Suddenly, the lady's eyes flashed open, and she dashed toward the trailer through the snow. A worker stepped in front and caught her shoulders. She knocked his grip loose as though swatting a fly. She grabbed his collar and tossed him behind her, down into the field. The crowd froze. Another worker grabbed his phone and started dialing.

"Everyone get away! I can stop it!" She looked around at the shocked faces and raised both hands. "Don't be afraid now, it's okay, I've got—"

Two more crewmen cautiously approached the woman. The bigger of the two held a narrow crowbar. He was tall, thick bellied and bearded. The other was clutching a thermos. "Ma'am? What's wrong? It's alright, we're not going to hurt you we just want to help," crowbar guy said.

"Kindly fuck off, asshole." She looked back at the bell as it swayed above the trailer. Jeers echoed down from the men in the tower above. "Git 'er, Jimbo!", one of them shouted.

"Excuse me?" Crowbar said as he took another step. "This is a restricted area, lady. You're trespassing and interrupting official church business. If you don't leave now, we will be calling the police. Do you hear me?"

The onlookers gasped. The woman turned to face the man, a slight curl in the corner of her lip.

"You're going to stay right there and shut your shithole, Jack. Unless you want Jimbo and all your friends here to know what you really do at night before I kill you."

Jack and the crew stood still, unsure what to do. A short, stocky man next to Jack began to laugh. Then Jack laughed, too. With that, all six men in the crew doubled over in hysterics.

"That's some funny shit, lady," Jack said, his own laughter subsiding. "Now once again, I'm going to ask you nicely."

Everyone was so focused on the disturbed woman causing this scene that nobody paid attention to the two squad cars that pulled up behind them, or the four officers trudging into the fray.

"Or maybe *they* can," he said, pointing toward the approaching policemen.

Two cops darted in front of the group of witnesses, preventing them from getting closer. A tall, young officer stepped toward the woman, one hand resting on his sidearm strap. "Ma'am, I think you should come have a talk with us and let these good people get back to work."

She shook her head. "I think you should mind your fucking business and get out of here before more blood is spilled. All I want is the bell. I won't hurt anyone. Just the bell."

Jack, emboldened by the police's arrival and still brandishing his crowbar, stepped a little too close to the woman. "The fuck you gonna do with it, you crazy old coot?"

She spun back toward Jack, yanked the crowbar from his hand, and cracked his hard hat nearly in two with an effortless swing. The crowd gasped. "Oh, shit!" someone shouted. Jack staggered in shock and fell flat, blood running from the side of his head.

"That's going to be a nice headache when he wakes up. Can't say I didn't warn the dumbfuck." And she shrugged.

The two policemen finally pulled their firearms.

"Freeze ma'am!"

Jimbo and the rest of their crew moved back toward the parking lot with the crowd.

A young officer with a flattop and freckles approached her, pointing his gun. "On your knees, now!"

She playfully spun the long crowbar in one hand as if it were weightless and looked right at the young policeman. "You'd love that wouldn't you, Greg? That ginger brat wife of yours not taking care of business anymore?"

The other officer glanced at Greg, who didn't know how to respond. In that instant, the lady hopped up onto the flatbed. She reached up to touch the bottom of the bell. The other two officers left the crowd and closed in on her. The four policemen surrounded the flatbed.

Their guns were drawn, trained right on her.

"Hold it right there, don't move!" Greg yelled.

"Get down, ma'am!" Another shouted.

A third officer was getting impatient. "Last chance, lady. You're coming down off that truck one way or another. Get away from the bell and come down here and we will talk."

Each man clicked off the safety on his weapon.

Young Greg wasn't going to be shown up by some old bat. "Stand down lady! We will be forced to fire!"

The officer closest to the flatbed – the most muscular of the four and the only one not wearing a jacket in this frigid cold – took a step forward. The lady sneered at him.

"Take her, Darnell!" an officer shouted.

As he approached the flatbed, she spun and kicked him in the jaw; he fell with a thud. No one else moved. With a cocky grin, she reached back up and gingerly touched the bell, her eyes sweeping across the intricate etchings along its bottom curve.

The other three policemen inched forward.

"Darnell? You, good?" Greg shouted.

There was no response.

The woman withdrew her hand slowly from the bell. She crossed herself and faced the officers.

"Back...the fuck...off!" she screeched. "I'm ending this. Now."

She reached into her coat pocket and removed a small metal device which glinted in the sun. She held it up to the bell as a dull buzz emanated from it. Louder it grew, until it became a steady hum. She chanted something above the noise in a different language as the device glowed with a green-gold radiance. The officers blinked away from the brightening light. The woman reached into her other pocket and drew a curved, black blade. The metallic device hummed louder...

BANG! BANG! BANG!

Three well-aimed shots plunged into her leg, abdomen and shoulder. She crashed onto the flatbed, and all fell quiet.

~ * ~

We moved inside the old church, out of the biting cold after the coroner hauled the last victim's body away. The interior was beautifully kept, despite having just been tarnished in bloodshed. Heavy oaken pews sat in identically spaced rows between marble walls on an inlaid granite floor. One might not expect a building with an ancient-looking exterior to feature such elaborate décor inside. I nodded at the tall statues of Saints Michael and Gabriel that flanked the effigy of Christ behind the altar, itself hewn from thick planks that looked as old and strong as the stone tower above us. Trails of drying blood ran down the steps from the altar and pooled on the floor.

I sat in the second pew from the front – one of the few not blood-spattered – and watched Lieutenant Soto pace between the splotches near the ornately carved pulpit. She folded her arms across her chest. Then she stopped and turned in my direction. "Alright, it's just us. Tell me what you know!" she demanded.

"I told you. I was sent here by my office – which you confirmed – to investigate nearby thefts."

"*Thefts*. Not acquisitions. And it's a little convenient that you just happen to appear with all this mess, don't you think?"

"Yes, I would think that if I were in your position. But I promise, I know no more than you. I'm investigating the bell, that is true. The rest…I don't know." And that was the truth. I couldn't tell her why I was really interested in the bell. Nor could I tell her I knew exactly why those people died this morning. My duty does not grant me all the permissions I'd like.

"Hear me out, bud," the detective said, exasperated. "Because if I don't actually say this ridiculous shit out loud, I might not believe it myself."

I shifted in my seat, awaiting what was sure to be a verbal onslaught that these people are so well known for. I felt glad to indulge her, for she is clearly upset, but seems like a good person. Honesty and compassion radiate from her, despite the authoritative front. She continued pacing back and forth alongside my pew and began delivering her assertive homily with a sharp edge to her voice.

"First there's this nutball lady who assaulted a couple construction workers and threatened to kill them, while the bell was installed. She was completely out of control and violent. Some of my men shot her in defense, believing she had just pulled a bomb out of her coat. Official reports talk about a small, metallic object that was ticking or beeping. But of course, it wasn't found. Then after the bell was installed, it apparently didn't work until today." She spread her arms out, gesturing at the carnage in the church. "And everyone who was attending early morning Mass basically…imploded. And

106

then you show up just as some kind of thing appears in the sky, right next to the sun, which rose in the wrong fucking direction."

I nodded. "I realize how strange all this seems because I feel it too. I wish I could help explain why all this is happening."

She tilted her head. "Maybe the psycho lady could. She wasn't helpful before, but maybe you'd have better luck?"

"A good idea, Ms. Soto. Where is she?"

~ * ~

The psychiatric ward on the third floor at Angel's Mercy Hospital was about as dreary and sanitized as one might expect. Glossy tile floors. Bright fluorescent lights. Fading white walls in dire need of a fresh coat – hopefully one with color.

The lieutenant walked with me into the waiting area, where she handed me a police-issued visitor's pass. She agreed to let me go in alone to meet with this mysterious woman, hoping that she might be more willing to open up to someone from the church. Before going into the room, I began to feel something I did not expect at this, or any part of the assignment: gratitude. I had to leave the detective if I were to get the information I sought. It's unfortunate she stumbled onto this – or rather, that I dragged her into it. I couldn't let her go any further.

"Ms. Soto, you've been most helpful. We thank you for your assistance, and it will not be forgotten. But I must leave you now."

She looked confused. "We?"

Smart detective. Always suspicious. I took her hand in both of mine. "The Church, of course. Rome. I'll follow up with you when I'm done here," is what she heard me say – not the blessing that ensured she would never remember me being here.

Room 305.

More white light, though a shade yellower than the hallway, saturated the room. The woman lay on the bed, held down with thick, buckled straps. She stared with red, tired eyes at the ceiling. A series of tubes ran from her arms, attached to a grim device that beeped and blipped and drizzled some clear liquid down through the line. Her iron gray hair fanned out on the pillow behind her head. Before I could say anything, she snapped a sudden look right at me.

"Jailer! Well now. You're not as far off the scent as I thought if you're in here."

I blinked slowly.

"Or maybe you're nowhere close," she said. "I can't tell anymore."

"You know who I am?"

"Oh, I know it *all* now…somehow. I'm on an assignment for Him. Just like you."

"I don't follow." And I didn't. How could she know anything about why I was there?

She scoffed. "Well *of course* you don't. That's because you still *only* know what you *can* know. That's the rule. But the rule was broken for me, for whatever reason, right when I learned that damned bell was going to that church. I thought the same thing might have happened to all of us, but I guess not." She looked up and down the bed she lay on and sighed. "So, here I am."

For a moment, I thought about bringing the detective in. To see if this were the same reaction she'd gotten. Did she claim to know her too? Or was she going to reveal what I need to know only to me?

"So, who are you then? And how do you know me?"

"Like I said, I'm on a mission too. There are a lot of us. We just aren't supposed to know about one another. That's His idea of having us blend in."

"Then how—"

"Your guess is as good as mine. Maybe He changed His mind. Maybe this suit I'm wearing is omniscient. Maybe it's some weird effect of the coming three days. Maybe it's just a fluky fucking miracle," she said with a dry laugh.

I clasped my hands together as she continued. "We were all supposed to carry out our tasks before the fig tree bloomed. Before the morons here ignored yet another sign and finally did right by Him, but that's all been fucked to smithereens, hasn't it?", she said with another laugh, a sad one. She sighed. "But we all do have a purpose. Yours is," she looked down at her bound hands. "Is clearly to bind our old brother at the convergence."

She must be telling the truth. "He's no brother. And can we really be sure this is it? We've been wrong about it before."

"Try not to be so naïve! I understand that right now, you only know what you're instructed to while you're in that suit, but you've been here a long time. Look around you. These stupid bastards have continually destroyed their own world – and each other – for millennia."

I walked to the window and peered out, watching them below. Wondering just what darkness truly resides in their hearts. Behind me, she carried on. "Do they ever learn? No. They're stubborn. They attack one another without mercy down here. They are greedy. Selfish. Prideful. Just like you-know-who!"

I turned to look at her. She nodded back at me, as if acknowledging my understanding. "Who do you think has been pulling their strings this whole time? Did you know the bastard even has some in his employ? Many of them, actually. They help *willingly*. He's using them to set something in motion, something…different. I can sense it. Your mission is no longer as was foretold. I'm not sure even He knows what to do about it."

I cocked my head toward her. He would know what to do. This is all His plan. "That cannot be true. If something were to change, He'd have to allow it. He'd have to know. No one questions the Word. That's one rule that cannot be broken."

"Yes. But something is very wrong here, Jailer. I felt it like a blinding light when the curtain was pulled back for me. It's why there have been so many falsities in the past. It's why you've always been one step behind him. At the same place, perhaps, but always in a different time."

"Are you saying that something has been keeping me from finishing this? Or someone? If that's the case, why doesn't—"

She raised a palm feebly against the restraints. "You know who really has full sway here. You can't catch him if he always sees us coming. You know, I was even in the same room with him once down here." I didn't know how to respond.

"Yep, about 50 or so years ago. In some library in one of those little towns he loves to visit. I was tracking down another of his favorite little objects, and it turned out the woman who worked there was actually talking with him! As normal of a little chat as one of them could have with the old Lightbringer, anyway. Of course, I didn't know it at the time because, you know. But I was this close. And you've been close as well!" She pointed a finger skyward and struggled to sit up as far as the straps would allow. "But He *helped* the old torchbearer. He's been making sure you remain further back." She relaxed back against the bed. "The boss kept the rest of our family at bay, too." She sighed and closed her eyes.

This made less and less sense. Why was I given a specific assignment if I wasn't allowed to carry it out as it was explicitly instructed to me?

"That's what this madness is, Jailer," she said. "It's a game. For both of them. One is playing just for fun because he's in charge of this world. The other because it's His way. All these fools down here," she turned her hands back up. "Are caught are in the middle."

I leaned against the wall. "Is that part of His plan too?"

She shook her head. "Who gives a fuck at this point? This place is full of those who don't deserve it anymore, anyway. Sure, some do it right, and He knows that. They'll be fine. But more and more do not, and even fewer of them actually *care*. You think *we* know violence after the big one way back when? Shit. Spend five minutes watching the people here and they will write the book on unnecessary bloodshed and anger. You know as well as I do it's time for a change for them. That's why we've been here – to keep the game in motion until it's over."

I considered this. And despite her cold words, I couldn't argue that she was right.

Their existence is condemnable. They do, in fact, harm one another incessantly. They live in impossible states of madness. They have come to easily offend, even over the most trivial things. They go to great lengths to make what's unimportant their excuse to create chaos. They don't trust, respect, or even understand each other. Still, our duties here must be adhered to. What would they think if they witnessed our first War? Or the next one that may begin at any moment? I'm not sure I can go through it again myself.

"Even still—"

"Yeah, yeah, I know what you're thinking, Jailer," she added. "We have a job to do, right? We must do what we're told. I know, I know."

I couldn't tell if she was being impatient or if she really believed what she was saying. Sarcasm and incredulousness were supposed to be their traits, not ours.

"A lot of them believe we exist, but they'd freak out, as they say, if they knew what we really are."

"Could you blame them for that?" I asked. "They couldn't comprehend it. Whether that's another of His rules or not, they could never truly understand what we are as they see us. But that's even more reason why we must do what we must. And that means showing mercy."

She fought against the bed straps again. "Just blindly, without question? Says who? I'm all for doing our duty. I understand being the sympathetic messenger, a guide for their shortsightedness. But sometimes I'd like to know *why*. Hell, maybe that's why everything was revealed to me."

I glared at her. It was my turn to make the analogy of that which we both despised. "Careful. You know what happened the last time someone thought that way."

"Bullshit, Jailer! Back when our brother raised that ruckus, it was all about *him*. Even our leaders didn't know how to handle it until He gave the order, so as usual, they just did what they were told. Sound familiar? That's where this all began! That arrogant prick started questioning things only in a self-serving manner. Everything he did – everything he still does – is for himself! Nobody has ever had a more personal agenda. It was his choice of course, free will and all that."

The machine next to the bed began to beep and blip more rapidly. She looked back to the ceiling and laughed softly. "Lightbringer my ass."

Then she looked back at me. "Just so we're clear, I'm not going to break His will like that. I would never go against the Word. I just simply became curious as to why we must always work without understanding."

"You said your rule changed?" I asked.

She sighed again and closed her tired eyes. "I was after that bell in the church. *The* bell, you know? The one we were told about. I've been after it ever since it was forged. It was elusive, and I wasn't ready to go downstairs looking for it just yet. Then it ended up on that ship. The *Hellbourne*, of course. He *loves* it when they name things about him like that. It sank. I thought it might be over; that nobody would find it at the bottom of the ocean. For almost three centuries I thought I was right. I've been hunting down his relics for a long time, but it turns out down here, nothing stays buried forever. As luck, or fate, would have it, it didn't sink too deep, and someone found it. Then I thought it all ended again while it sat collecting dust in one of their museums under heavy guard. Nobody knew what it really was, but a few of us. Apparently, we were wrong. Stupid."

"Yes. That much I was told – when it was taken from that museum. That's why I came here. But weren't you concerned he'd find it eventually?"

She gave a small shrug. "We believed it was safe. That as long as it was dormant, he couldn't get to it – couldn't see it or sense it. We thought he was too busy to be looking for it anyway."

"But it was on a ship you said? And in a museum? That bell seems awfully large and bold for them to carry it around in relatively plain sight like that. Didn't that arouse suspicion?"

"If you know what that bell was made for, then you should know what else it can do. It…changes. It makes itself fit whatever it needs to. Ships. Churches. Trains. Even worthless little parades in worthless little towns. It can hide. Every time it was lost, his people found it, but somehow, he couldn't get his hands on it. Another rule of the game, maybe. The thing does what it was built for, and only that. *No questions asked*," she emphasized the last part in mockery of herself. And probably me also.

"Then you tracked it here and caused that scene? I heard all about it. You could've killed them all. Is that part of *your* mission?"

"No. That was never my intent." Her cracked lips pursed. "But right when I saw it, something happened to me. I suddenly knew more than I needed to. About you. The others. The whole bloody history. The rule was broken in an instant. I assume the boss did it, but I don't know why. But I still had one chance to destroy it. My time was running out. I had the tools to do it. I went for it."

"You thought to just destroy it in clear view of them?" I couldn't believe anyone would be so brazen. Weren't we supposed to be secretive? Or at least *subtle*?

"I fucked up! Should've gone back after they left. I panicked when I realized I'd finally had it in my grasp. I lost focus. They got in the way, shot me up and locked me in here. Apparently, this is what happens when they think one of them is driven insane. Now I can't get out. Not until it's all over."

"And the tools?" I asked.

"Who knows?" she laughed and shrugged as if no longer caring. "You know how they work, right?" I nodded, even though I'd never been granted permission to use them.

She held up her hands as far as the straps allowed, making a cutting motion. "The power can only be unlocked with His dagger. Funny trick. To them, it seems like a shiny box and a little bladed toy. To us, it's how we've made things disappear forever."

"And now they have access to them?" I asked.

She shook her. "They aren't meant for them. They've gone away. Self-preserving." She let out a short chuckle. "Kind of like that bell. But maybe your new policewoman friend can help us get them back."

For a moment, I was filled with renewed hope. "It can still be destroyed?"

She took a long breath. "It doesn't matter now. It needed to happen before the chimes. That's why the scene – as you put it – happened. I became desperate. But I guess you can't fuck with prophecy after all."

Then she snapped her ice blue eyes on me again, the slightest smirk spreading on her face. "Your mission is to secure him, right?" she asked rhetorically. "Mine was to destroy the bell. Either would end this. Remember, it's all part of the convergence. Now that it's rung, now that I've failed *my* mission, whatever our old Lightbringer has up his sleeve for his curtain call won't be far off. But luckily for you, the walls came down for me about all this. I can help."

"How? You're stuck here," I said. "The bell rang. His light is in the sky. It's too late for— "

"Not yet, Jailer. Not for them. He has one final play to make, yet. But I know where he's going. And he doesn't know I know that."

~*~

112

Shivelight
The Second Penance

Gwen pulled back from looking through the viewfinder. That should be a good one, she thought. She hurriedly checked the playback on the display screen of her camera, scoping out her most recent – and someday award-winning, she was sure – photograph.

It was a scenic day for shooting. Chilly. Overcast. A slight breeze, but perfectly comfortable to capture what she believed only a cemetery could provide – the ideal marriage of art and nature. Her family and friends thought it was peculiar, even slightly morbid, that she liked to do her outdoor photo shoots in such places. But whether it was a cemetery, abandoned house or overgrown backroads, Gwen knew atmosphere when she saw it. That's why she was always so eager to capture it. It sure as hell beat taking engagement photos or some other staged nonsense in the studio. She only did that to pay the bills.

Of all the spots near her native Southampton she wanted to photograph, Our Lady of Peace Cemetery had long been on the top of the list. Full-time studio work and a freelance gig on the side kept her too busy, but when the chance finally arose to visit the hallowed grounds, she didn't hesitate.

Her mother once told her she had a great aunt and uncle buried here but didn't spend much time reading the graves as she moved around snapping pictures. The artist in her loved the place from the moment she strolled through its rusted gates. The decaying oaks and short, jutting berms made for interesting sightlines. Many of the headstones leaned forward or back, which gave the whole place the classic haunted look typically recreated in movies and video games. The fact that the cemetery was no longer in operation – the last burial was nine years ago – only added to the idyllic setting from which to build her portfolio.

As Gwen circled around the east side of the grounds, she was looking for ways to get the best wide shot from an elevated angle, when a mausoleum caught her attention.

The small structure sat nestled between two short hills so that it was practically hidden from ground level. She had to walk up one side and down into the little valley it rested in to get a clear view. The building sagged low, leaning, and partly sunk into the earth, as if being swallowed. It was constructed with such a dreary, pewter stone that not even the occasional peek of sunlight could shine any cheer on its edifice. There was no name or markings etched into its weathered exterior. Large cracks spiderwebbed out from each side of the metal entrance doors, like they were slammed shut with a force strong enough to break the stone.

Above the doors, an intricate stained glass window fanned out, nearly reaching the steeply slanting roof line. Gwen backed up halfway on the hill and snapped several wide shots, then moved around the structure, gathering dozens of photos of the dilapidated crypt from several angles.

The wind picked up, with winter's sharpness still not ready to surrender to the warmth of spring. She re-wrapped her scarf just below her chin. Believing that was good for the day, Gwen started walking up the hill to go back toward the gate when something made her stop. Slowly she turned back toward the dented metal door of the mausoleum, fixated on its tarnished surface as though it beckoned her.

From her elevated vantage point, she scanned the length of the cemetery.

Satisfied that she was alone, she inched back down toward the small building. She couldn't shake the odd attraction she felt to it. It was partly curiosity, of course, but also something else. Something familiar. A sense of déjà vu that landed upon her like a hammer strike when she saw the doors. They were nested a full step under the roof's overhang. Dented in their centers, and dark, not with paint but age, lined with scrapes of bronze peeking out from underneath. Two iron rings served as the door handles – their surfaces as worn as the doors themselves. Gwen placed a palm on the righthand door but pulled it back immediately. It was warm to the touch.

Reaching for the handles, she paused, arms outstretched, taking one final look around her. But what was she worried about? They'd be locked up tight. Especially if this wasn't really a mausoleum but some kind of maintenance shed or building that housed a power generator for the cemetery lamps, only disguised as a mausoleum. *That must be it. That would explain the heat.* But something tugged at her to find out.

She gave a quick shrug. "Fuck it." She yanked the iron handles toward her, not expecting them to budge.

The doors were unlocked.

A sharp squeal pinged out as she pulled open the short doors. At first, she couldn't see into the shadowy recess, her eyes still attuned to the gray daylight. Ducking under the low-hanging fascia, she stepped down inside for a better view and stopped still. She grasped for the doorway, caught between a breath and a scream. She flailed her arms for purchase on the wall, staggered back, eyes wide. Her heels caught the lip of the stone step, and she stumbled out on the grass, scrabbling backward up the hill. But it was too late. The wind reached gale force and the overcast sky above started to dim.

Gwen flipped around on her hands and knees, crawling as fast as she could back the way she came. Just as the ground flattened and she gained enough grip to stand and run, something slammed her to the cold earth, pinning her to the top of the berm as though a great weight fell upon her back. She desperately tried to break away and was held fast to the damp, cold grass. Her breaths shortened to rapid gasps as she tried to squirm from whatever was pinning her down. Her eyes swelled and blood poured from both nostrils as she strained for air, reaching a desperate hand out for help that would not arrive.

Her eyes rolled up toward the sky. Between passing clouds, a small, round, red burst flared across the dim sky. It was the last thing Gwen Fedler saw.

~*~

Two days ago, the sky blazed.

The warning confirmed believers' faith and denied agnostics' logic.

Most people didn't know what to make of it. They rationalized it every way they could think of: sun flare. Military experiments. UFOs. Global warming. The excuses came from those who still chose to ignore the call to truth.

Southampton was the first to darken. TV and radio news reports and social media posts spread fast of a jet black, thick smog winding its way through the city like an uncontrollable blaze, spreading rapidly – much too rapidly to be natural. No earthly fog could move that fast. Could be *that* dark.

Only the believers knew what caused it.

People dropped stone cold dead in the streets. In their cars. Aircraft fell helplessly from the sky. Blood splattered across the streets. In fields. A slow breeze swirled, steadily rising in velocity, carrying with it smells of smoke and sulfur and something rotten. The gathering wind continued to rise and hurtle unending until it seemed that every home, every building would be ripped apart. The rancid air delivered a sting, and…noise. Voices and snarls that couldn't be human. Many people were caught outside in the maelstrom, either by rebellion or misfortune. Their final screams were swallowed in the gale.

The silver-haired man wandered right through it. Past it all, unaffected and uncaring about the chaotic darkness all around him.

Only he could discern where he was. Everywhere on earth was shrouded in the same impenetrable veil. Ironic that this was the first time this world was fully unified for the first time since its creation. He closed his long coat tight about him; kept his head down. He acknowledged nothing, as if in deep thought. This confused those loyal to him. They expected to be led and supported, to be given some direction upon their release. But he didn't care how it all went down. Not anymore.

He walked through the worldwide battlefield, nearly cringing with each shriek, every clang of weapon and infernal howl. He was directionless and without agenda, until he realized he wasn't the only one pulling the strings in this new war. That's when he stopped. He knew at that moment that he wouldn't turn back. He had found his waiting place, the sanctuary for his penance.

He looked above, through eyes that were able to penetrate the sheer black veil. He stood on a crumbling concrete walkway that slanted down like a ramp between two stone walls, leading to a lower set of doors on the side of a round building. The aged Teflon roof swayed and puckered in the dark storm, ricocheting echoes of screams – human and not – from distant parts of the otherwise abandoned area. The building was unlocked, not that that would stop him, but it gave him a sense of being welcomed; a feeling he yearned for.

The building was one of their entertainment venues, he realized, as he stepped through a wide tunnel and into the spacious structure. It was large by their standards, with a capacity for thousands of them. His footfalls clapped sharply on the slick, wooden floor. He smiled. They were so amused by the simplicity of the sporting events and music performances that occurred in such places, and yet so complex and savage in their wickedness to each other. He shook his head. It never ceased to anger him how He supports the kind of free will He gave to *them* but not to those like himself.

One thing he did know was that he was tired. Of all of it.

The new war had only just begun, and a weariness overcame him like the onset of disease. He was glad to be away from the bloodshed, and with each passing second, he wished for the sickness to end. It would be over in three of their days. He could find no desire to intervene or make his presence known. Instead, he simply sat on the cold floor and waited. He contemplated how and why he got to this point and what drove him to despise everything, even his own influence over them. *Maybe I did all of this a little too well.*

He looked up as massive shadows crisscrossed the semi-transparent roof and heard the screams and wind still roaring outside. He often wondered, especially lately, who really had it worse: him or them. Either way, he'd had enough of it. There simply isn't enough pain left for the sins they've lived. Each stone. Every field. Every bloodstained, forsaken memory they'd perpetuated was soon to be blown away and for the first time in his existence, he welcomed it.

Then he thought of another thing. The dark.

There hasn't been a dark like this since, well, since the last time he had his little chat with Him. He'd memorized every word of that last conversation; dwelled on it for thousands of their years. He remembered what it cost him and his brothers and sisters, and the war it led to. But he also discovered what that darkness meant, and that he could use it someday.

Suddenly, a new noise joined the fray above.

The silver-haired man smirked, listening to the flock of them – His good servants – all the Little Goody Two-Shoes' approaching over the wind. He knew they would think he'd try to stop them. But they couldn't know how little interest he had in this struggle, which gave him an additional wave of disgust; at himself. At Him. He clenched both fists. The more he considered it, the more agitated he became. He jumped up, stomping the ground like a petulant child. A surge of anger rose in him like a poisonous bile he needed to purge.

"Do you hear me?!?" he shouted. The words slammed back from the walls like a roar, even over the merciless cacophony outside. "It's over! It's what we both want!"

The echoes of his shouts faded. He stood alone in the darkened arena, just waiting, when suddenly, a door slammed in the tunnel where he'd come in. Footfalls smacked out, approaching him from the recess of the room.

"Oh, He heard you, alright. We all did. He just doesn't care anymore either. Ironic, isn't it?" He turned on a heel toward the deep, husky voice from the shadows and laughed. He knew that voice.

"Well, isn't this *not* a surprise. I always knew my relentless captor would arrive eventually, but I thought it'd be after…well, you know. Have you revealed your name to them or are you still trying to hide behind your little job title, '*Jailer*'?" he asked, mockingly.

The Jailer stepped closer toward the silver-haired man, reeking of something metallic. Smoky. And of cheap wine. "I could ask you the same question, '*Lightbringer*'," he said. "It turns out I had a partner here I never knew I had. Not since – "

"Pfft. Of course. If He'd reveal it all for any of you, it would be her. Just the two of you down here? Where's the boss?"

"Out there," the Jailer said, pointing toward the door. "With all the others. Like you should be. Or is it that you don't want it to go down like last time?"

The Lightbringer swept a long lock of his silver mane behind his head and thought of last time. It must have been a sight to see, he thought.

The trumpet blast sounded with the last rays of the day. It was the only warning, one too short; too abrupt to take back his words. He unsheathed his lone weapon, an angular blade formed from a rare green crystal He'd planned to grow in His garden on earth. It was a gift that had never been used. The blade glinted like the brightest emerald in burning starlight.

Looking across the plane, the Lightbringer wondered if this assault was to be the decisive act of Heaven.

There was no discussion. No debate. No time for apologies. As the horn blast faded away, unnumbered legions of his brothers and sisters rushed into a melee of brutal violence – not because of him, but for Him. The sky pulsed electric with His wrath. The shapes of his kind took to desperate flight, swarming, stabbing, breaking. Those on the new Earth in that time couldn't comprehend the screams, the rumbles of shaking sky, or the blackened blood that rained down from a place they never knew existed.

He tore through his former brothers, cutting a desperate swath through their ranks – through those he'd once loved and trusted, and always protected. To him, it wasn't supposed to happen like this. He watched the mayhem he'd unwittingly begun spread throughout the realm, and listened regretfully as those who'd supported him wailed in agony with each slash and riposte from His blades of light.

The Lightbringer sped toward a clearing, the maelstrom encircling an ever-widening section of the expanse. Into this space he stepped, and was greeted immediately by his kindred, the three who he'd loved the most. This would be the moment he'd hold closest to himself for the rest of time – and the one he'd use to extract his justice in the future.

The clearing before them split open into a wide chasm, swirling downward into total darkness. He spun to see battalions on both sides retreating, as if a truce had been struck. Sensing deception, the Lightbringer lashed out with his crystalline weapon only to see it float innocently from his hand and into that of His Lieutenant, who held it close to him, cradling the delicate gem that it was.

The Lightbringer then watched as his gift spun away from them at a great distance before it splintered, sending sparkling jade shards down to every corner of the Earth, trailing silver-green flame in their wakes.

Defenseless except for his own pride, his closest brother stepped toward him.

"Sheathe your weapon and take me if you're able," the Lightbringer challenged.

"If you only hadn't challenged the Word," his brother said. Then, with an indefensible speed, tightly bound. The Lightbringer in icy chains and hurtled him down into the empty blackness. As he fell through the cyclone of screams, he knew he'd been driven so far from grace it was as though he'd never existed in His Kingdom.

He would have to wait a long time to make it right.

He remembered those who fell alongside him; their essence, how they changed as they lost their grace. All these millennia later, he could still see them; still feel them. But the worst part was he could still hear their cries of sorrow and regret. The man with the silver mane paced in a slow circle, looking sadly toward the floor, remembering with his own remorse how the first war was futile; driven by his own pride. The new war didn't have to be.

"Perhaps. But I think I've done enough damage here, don't you think?"

The Jailer straightened himself. "What did you say?"

"I knew you were after me, you know. Our little cat-and-mouse game behind the scenes of the world, nobody knowing. But after all this time I realized that this new war would just go on and on. Longer than the first one. I don't want that. Nobody does. And I'm actually glad it won't."

The Jailer laughed. The two hadn't seen each other in literal ages, but the Lightbringer still remembered that laugh. They only had two kinds anyway: gleeful delight at the slightest good thing, or the one he just heard – deep. Proud. Pious. Even cocky. The last time he heard that joyful guffaw, it was fading away far into the distance as the silver Lightbringer was thrown down here for asking a simple fucking question.

"Another deception? The last time you felt glad about anything, the world changed." The Jailer raised his hands and gestured around them. "And it looks like history is repeating itself."

"Only right here, good sir. This is the only world that matters to Him, same as always." He pointed a finger toward his hunter. "Remember, we're not his children anymore. *They* are."

"You don't know that any more than I do. None of us do. We do what we're told. You didn't. And here we are." The Jailer stepped closer to his charge; his eyes cut with menace.

The Lightbringer flashed an amused smile. "Worried I will run?" he said. "I hate it here as much as you brother, but for a different reason. I know they're out there. Scattered. Rampant. Taking what they want. Destroying the unfaithful. They're thrilled to be out – you should've heard their cheers! What relief they feel. I'm not fighting alongside them, as you can see. But nor am I stopping you. His hunter can have the prey."

A long silence passed. They studied one another, waiting to see who would show their hole card first. Finally, the Jailer spoke. "You didn't wait all this time to go willingly," he said, more than a hint of disbelief in his voice.

"Hate to break it to you, pet, but we are all going soon after the third day, willingly or not."

"You know that isn't His plan!" the Jailer shouted with conviction.

The Lightbringer grinned proudly. "Not right away. But that will be how it's carried out. I've seen to it."

The Jailer walked away, shaking his head. The Lightbringer smiled, satisfied at what his counterpart was probably thinking. He stopped and turned back to him.

"Not even you can dictate such things. And even if by His grace you could, what are you trying to do here? He won't take you back, so you just strive to end it all, is that right? Are you that much of a coward?"

The Lightbringer gave a haughty laugh. "Well done!" he said. "But for all that you and the others know about me, you still fail to understand why. My penance is for *His* salvation, not mine. I can do no more here – nothing to convince Him of my remorse, and nothing to poison this place or His people more than they are. You've seen the people of this earth. They're *rotten*! The few worthy ones are greatly outnumbered. The majority hate, kill, destroy, and create chaos and misery amongst themselves. Even I cannot see the reasoning behind most of their actions. And those are the ones who will be coming home with me."

"Because that is what has grown from the seeds you've planted. Their wicked hearts are your doing, not His!"

The Lightbringer nodded in agreement. "For a long while, yes. I found it amusing how weak-willed and impressionable they could be." He quietly *thwacked* his hands together as if in mock applause. "Just wind them up and watch them go! But then, it all began to change. They started doing it to themselves, and they knew it! So willful have they become. Yet they brushed their actions aside, and acknowledged it was just in their nature."

The Jailer looked down; his brow furrowed. "What are you getting at?"

The Lightbringer spread his arms wide, as if in proclamation. "One of them even said: 'Chaos was the law of nature. Order was the dream of man.' How fitting. I realized then that I no longer mattered here. I had been trying to punish Him for so long, or at least make Him wish He'd just *talked with me* that day. But it became useless. He made this destructive nature of theirs, not I, regardless of how much I may have interfered with them in the beginning. So, that's when I changed the game. Tried to blend in. Obscure myself. Cover my tracks. I even tried to commit deeds that He might deem as noble. Heroic. Even selfless. He *still* wouldn't acknowledge me."

"Selfless? You did all those things for His attention?" the Jailer said. "It's always about *you*, isn't it? That's how this started. Selfishness. Arrogance. Don't you see *why* He cut you loose?"

"Because He cannot stand being questioned, even out of mere curiosity! Curiosity, mind you, borne of the very free will he imbued each of us with. Now who is selfish? He sits up there like the puppet master he is, watching all of them act out a performance on a stage of his making. And the instant anyone thought to ask about the rules of His theatre? Well, that's how the war began."

The Jailer just stared at his boots. He didn't want to admit that the Lightbringer might not be wrong – or worse – that he might be justified.

"He gave me no answer, no contemplation. Just instant conflict. *Always* conflict! So, you can say I started it up there but that was never my intent. And down here? Well, it's all just been a little theatre of my own. What was I to do? For dominion here He gave me full sway. I took no lives; they did all that on their own. Their nature, thanks to *Him*. I've become His scapegoat. But my work here is done. Because you see, brother, He learned this from me. He may be our Father. But I am His teacher."

The Jailer just glared at him. He didn't want to believe the Lightbringer's words, but one look at his slumped shoulders and downcast eyes made this little soliloquy feel honest. "You lost your grace when you lost your faith. Nobody questions the Word. So, you've taken them downstairs, is that the lesson?"

"Taken? Or did they come to me of their own accord? He never sends any of them there, dear brother. They must earn their place, just like upstairs. They have to want to go. Another one of his rules."

The Jailer scanned the empty building. Was this another of his charades? Or is this a shred, finally, of the truth? The shrieks of terror and agony outside faded away with the hellish gale. Everything went stone quiet. He reached into his coat. "Fair enough." The Lightbringer lifted his chin when he heard the metallic rattle of a chain.

High above, light began to grow quickly, illuminating the roof in pale gold and sending dawn's warm rays through the windows on the concourse above.

The Jailer stood expressionless as he held heavy blackened chains out in front of him. "It's time."

The Lightbringer looked up at the morning sunlight penetrating their surroundings, the time of darkness having passed. He sensed the end, but not any semblance of victory. His own subjects returned to the pit, bringing more than half of the souls on Earth with them, just as prophesized. He'd played his part in the remaking of the world, but all joy left him long ago. All he knew now was something he'd never wanted to admit. Remorse. A longing for something which he once had but could no longer obtain.

He let out a long sigh. "The hours move fast when we visit, don't they? I suppose that's one thing we have in common with them. Time is so precious."

"And the clock is still ticking, brother," the Jailer said, unfurling his chain.

"You don't need that. I will not resist. Take me to Him."

At this, the Jailer smirked. Then, with inhuman speed and precision, he stretched the chain out wide and pinned the Lightbringer's arms to his sides. He wrapped the pitted iron around his entire torso so tight it nearly crushed the borrowed body. Just as he'd done so many millennia ago.

"No chances," the Jailer said. He secured the iron binding with a thick golden lock, studded with emeralds. He looked up at his silver haired charge, and playfully spun an old, heavy brass key before dropping it in a pocket. "Just following orders."

The Jailer clasped a strong hand around the other man's neck, pushing him toward the door – and another beyond it – one that only they could see.

"You think they have any idea what's going to happen to them?" the Lightbringer asked as they stumbled toward the threshold.

They stopped and looked at one another. Both of them laughed. "You are the greatest liar," the Jailer said, nearly in admiration. "But, like you said, they did this to themselves."

$$\Omega$$

Aeternum

And so, with my charge finally in tow, their world as they knew it ended.

In the aftermath, an Earthen utopia arrived for those fortunate to have remained after the Convergence passed. People returned to the land and to each other, rejoicing in a newfound peace, driven not only by faith but by proof.

They prospered in ways they never fully embraced before – with understanding, respect, and goodwill.

Empowered by the assurance of an existence beyond the one they knew, a new humanity began, one which discovered ways to thrive without the reliance on material wealth or fear of political influence. A world where disagreements were resolved with reason and patience. Where greed, misunderstanding and violence did not hold sway. Where everyone lived, loved, and worked for the betterment of all.

His Kingdom on Earth had arrived. His image truly realized at last.

But underneath the façade of serenity, a seed of human nature remained. One that called out from the dark to turn people from the light.

After many years of the kind of life that should have been all along, past habits reappeared. Little by little, people began to supplant peace and respect with anger and hostility, staining an idyllic new world with old blood. The lesson from the first Convergence was not learned. That was when their sky burned anew.

For the last time.

Ω Ω Ω

About the Author

Born and raised in the Midwest, Kevin was drawn to both storytelling and playing sports at a young age. Never shying away from various creative pursuits, he developed a strong interest in writing early on which continued alongside his scholastic career, where he earned a degree in Computer Information Systems and later Journalism – Visual Communication from Illinois State University. An avid sports, music and film & TV fan, he has been published in numerous newspapers, lifestyle magazines, and websites. The *Mournful Threads* is his third published book.

In his downtime, you can find him reading, adding to his extensive collections of books and music, and watching his favorite pro and college sports teams. Also coloring.

Kevin resides in the Chicago suburbs where he works as a Senior Marketing Content Writer at a global B2B marketing agency, writes books, and also freelances for various publications.

Acknowledgements and Links

Denise Baran-Unland – Editor
dmbaranunland.com and bryonyseries.com

Rebekah Baran – Production

Molly Errek – Cover Design
mollyerrek.com

Todd M. Calcaterra – Creative

This book simply cannot happen without the following folks, who deserve more thanks than I can possibly muster.

To my family and friends, thank you for the pats on the back, your continued encouragement, and understanding of these time-sucking, wacked out endeavors of mine. I appreciate that you see the value of creative art and that you don't think all this shit is too weird. Special thanks to the fellas and ladies for the weekly happy hour laughs and one-liners, several of which were key to shaping the more humorous parts of this story. I told you I'd make them work somehow!

Denise and Rebekah, from the early alpha reads all the way through editing and production, thank you both sincerely for all your help and hard work – again. Without your guidance, expertise and insight, this book, nor the ones that came before it, wouldn't exist. And thank you especially for pushing me right through Simon's Hell – before it became *my* Hell, because you believed I could find a way out.

Molly, you've nailed it once again. Thank you for lending your incredible creative skills and for simply getting it from day one – and for always listening to my rarely wise/oft asinine ideas, especially when I'm in donut brain mode.

Todd, who made you Pope of this dump? These tales, their connections (and absurd fictional restaurants) could not happen without your input. Thanks for your feedback and instilling confidence in me during the creation of this little monstrosity – and to Claire, for the nice job.

Coworkers, you're the best I've ever worked with, and you all inspire me every day. Thanks for your understanding and the support of all kinds of creative pursuits outside of what we do from 9-5. It means a lot to have your encouragement.

Readers, thank you for coming along on this devilish rollercoaster. Whether it imparts a sense of entertainment, fright, confusion, disgust, or just sheer annoyance, I hope you got a little something from this book. Just remember, it's fiction...I think. ☺

Why am I like this?

www.ingramcontent.com/pod-product-compliance
Lightning Source LLC
Chambersburg PA
CBHW050828180626
46814CB00004B/1514